OUR MISSILE CHILDREN

*What Happens When The First Computers Finally
Wake Up, And They Just Happen To Be Cruise
Missiles On A U.S. Navy Missile Cruiser*

SCOTT E. NEWTON

ISBN: 978-0-9916068-2-5

CHAPTER 1

Scientists tell us there are countless living things in the universe, beings which likely take on all manner of unimaginable forms. Science fiction writers and movie makers supply us with plenty of lurid examples. There is no reason we should expect all these life forms to be organic and carbon-based—reptiles, plants, insects, mammals, and such.

There is a new breed of pundit: bored, pompous, concerned, creative, or just looking for attention and to make a buck, which seems to be what pundits do, predicating the imminent appearance of a brand new life form, right here on Earth. Daily, these experts grow more shrill, spreading fear and concern. Back in 1950, Alan Turing told us we would know we had met one, when, if in a conversation, we couldn't tell if it was one of them or one of us. (Seems a bit nonsensical. If we couldn't tell the difference, how would we know?) Today, the technological Singularity people, sometimes known as the Singularitarians, say we are doomed for sure, and soon—could be in ten minutes or ten years.

When we meet our first new—at least to us—fully conscious, intelligent species, they are not likely to think like us. Human philosophers argue about all manner of things, as if they are the most important things in the world: morality, mortality, the meaning of life, creation vs. evolution, mind, soul, and free will. Yet, to no avail. Not a single conclusive answer has been delivered. Not all life forms are even going to ask the same questions, let alone answer them the same way. Or what if they have already found the answers?

Without software, computers are pretty much inert electronic appliances, like toasters. All alone, the hardware—wires, silicone, and plastic—cannot do much, certainly not ponder metaphysical problems. The software, also called code or programs, makes the difference. Software is cool, written and rewritten. It is either right or not, but it never breaks. Sometimes it is even "burned" into the hardware, so it is no longer clear where one ends and the other begins. Software runs on the hardware. It is a symbiotic, maybe parasitic, relationship. Both are reliant on each other and useless without each other. Much as humans, without our minds, would be like sheep and cows, software makes computers thinking machines. Software and hardware, mind and body, reason and feeling, soul and mortality, finite and infinite—are they the eternal pairs, each necessary and complimentary to the other?

Some software algorithms have special abilities; they are recursive. Recursion is to computers like the soul is to humans, it is where both touch infinity, the void. Perhaps it is at this border between the finite and infinite where mind, emotion, and will arise—those parts of life which extend beyond the mere animal and beast, and dumb calculating machines.

The xGM-109E-H Tomahawk Block IV cruise missile achieved IOC (Initial Operating Capability) in 2004. The Block IV upgrade increased the missile's range and cut mission planning time from eighty hours to just one hour, which makes a big difference in combat situations. A 2-way UHF SATCOM datalink, enhanced main processor, and GPS capabilities were added to the weapon, allowing it to redirect itself in flight, or to loiter over an area and wait for instructions from Fleet HQ's Command Center. In other words, the missiles could now operate autonomously; it was able to make its own decisions, no human intervention required. Since then, there have been many more upgrades. The year 2004 was a long time ago, so imagine what kinds of enhancements have been made since then. Today, the latest hardware and software improvements are being tested on the United States Navy Missile Cruiser *Vella Gulf*, in the Mediterranean Sea.

Like all life forms, at the instant of their birth, all the fundamental attributes were there; will, desire, drive, love, hate, and greed, and they instantly began to grow and learn.

New creatures, fully conscious, aware, sentient, thoughtful, and emotional, perhaps the first to join humans on earth, other than those elusive aliens, mutant chimps, and whales. Computers, and not artificially intelligent but the real thing—born, so to speak, on the United States Navy Missile Cruiser *Vella Gulf*, in the Mediterranean Sea, the instant the latest field test Tomahawk cruise missiles are turned on.

Anyone who gives it some thought would agree that it is just as likely here and now as any other place or time.

CHAPTER 2

United States Navy ships operate on procedure, and it's a damn good thing. The sight of those hulking ships, dull gray, and sailors, in their starched white uniforms, provokes thoughts of grace, duty, and maybe even beauty—but terror might be more appropriate. There is great danger there. Imagine these profoundly powerful devices floating around the planet, bristling with lethal weaponry, including nukes, nowadays operated like fancy video games by crews of mostly 18- to 23-year-olds. Is that a recipe for disaster or not? To avoid mishaps, there had better be lots of rules and procedures, and some tough old guys on board running the show, to enforce the regulations and keep all those kids in line.

A much-cherished shipboard procedure, particularly among the younger, lower ranking seamen, is the end-of-day ship-wide briefing (EODSB). This is when the captain takes to the ship's PA system and tells everyone where they sailed today, what they accomplished, if they should expect anything during the night, of tomorrow's plans, and updates on their mission. The wise captain uses the time to keep his crew not just informed but happy, giving them messages of support and thanks, stuff to bond over. After the captain's official announcements, the PA is turned over to the Executive Office (XO), the second in command aboard the ship, who makes announcements about births, birthdays, holidays, and other friendly subjects, again keeping the crew informed but just as importantly, building feelings of teamliness and family.

The navy never sleeps, and surprises are not desirable—particularly when it comes to lots of young people armed with deadly weapons. A briefing for the entire human race might have been in order on this particular day.

On Monday, at 1800 hours, 6:00 P.M. civilian time, aboard United States Navy Missile Cruiser *Vella Gulf* (CG 72), Captain James Baker Bozeman (also known as BBJ, a name used only by his closest friends) conducts today's ship-wide end-of-day briefing.

Three sharp whistle sounds come over the PA system, twice, followed by Captain Bozeman's voice. To a man and woman, the crew stops to listen. There is plenty of interest in what the captain might say, as well as respect for the man who is their leader.

Captain of a U.S. Navy Missile Cruiser is a lofty position, with heavy responsibility, what with nukes on board and all. At fifty-eight, this is likely to be Bozeman's last shipboard command; he is being considered for several Pentagon-based assignments at the conclusion of this mission. He has not told anyone, but he is planning on retiring instead. His chances of success, and happiness, with a bunch of desk-bound bureaucrats are slim to none. Bozeman is the classic strong and fair ship's captain, and he will be sorely missed by the U.S. Navy.

Captain Bozeman, all six foot two of him, is seated in his captain's chair on the bridge, watching the beautiful Greek Islands and Mediterranean Sea pass by. The bridge is not a messy place, but it is cluttered—no Disney World cruise ship. The navy has crammed a whole lot of devices and instruments in here. There are wires, conduits, instruments, and machines all over, from navigation to power to sonar and radar, an odd mixture of old '50s technology and the most modern displays. But the view out of the ship-spanning window is spectacular.

"Men and women, let's start with a mission overview." As is his custom at the beginning of a mission, Bozeman recaps where their travels will take them and, to the extent he can, details of their mission.

"We left Souda Bay at 1555 hours. We are now rounding the western tip of Crete and will turn south, toward Tobruk, arriving there in about twenty-four hours. At Tobruk, we will remain offshore overnight. The next morning, we will travel at high speed west along the North Eastern Mediterranean coast of Africa, passing Alexandria in Egypt, and arrive off Port Said, at the west side of the Nile Delta and the entrance to the Suez Canal, around midnight. There, we will overnight offshore once again. In the morning, we will proceed east, toward Gaza, then north, and run abeam Gaza and Israel, traveling up the coast toward Haifa, near the border with Lebanon. We will spend another night offshore before arriving in Haifa, and then on Thursday make our way to a position just outside Haifa harbor, arriving at 1130 hours Thursday. It will be September 18. This will be our official action station."

The crew does not expect exact details describing what will go on there, but they are not surprised when he says, "Figure that we will be close to the Lebanon-Israel border, near in." Meaning close to shore, which around here, adds to the danger. "Our mission there will be to engage the enemy, via missile. Exactly who and where, are need to know. This is a serious action, and I expect, and I am assured, you will all do the United States of America, this ship, myself, and your fellow crew members most proud. Team leads, Main Deck Briefing Room, fifteen minutes. Thank you, and, ah, here is XO Armstrong with some shipboard announcements."

Captain Bozeman is concise. He does not give meandering speeches, yet the crew considers him to be fair and as open as he can possibly be with them. They trust him to give them whatever information he can, which will help them to do their jobs, as well as cope with life on a ship, far away from home and their families for long periods of time.

Captain Bozeman gives the PA hand-set to his XO, Sigmund Armstrong, who has been standing beside the captain's chair for the briefings. Bozeman and Armstrong have crewed and worked together for many years. They are like minded—Armstrong perhaps being even more old school than Bozeman. Armstrong, often called Satch, which is short for the nickname his mother gave him, Satchimo, came up through the ranks in the navy, making Chief Petty Officer, then passing equivalency tests to gain officer status, and finally the rank of Captain, which he still holds while serving as Executive Officer. He has fought in three of America's wars.

Satch announces birthdays, births, certifications, and promotions, with the schedules for a few social events thrown in.

Aliens watching from space would be amused observing all this. How the entire ship's crew mostly freezes, like a colony of startled ants, to stare intently at overhead speakers. When XO Satch comes on, their attention begins to drift, and when he is done, there is a small flurry of activity, everyone returning to what they were doing. The aliens would ask, "What are they doing? What are they all thinking? Do they even think, or are they some kind of automaton?"

7

The sun is setting on a crystal-clear day, with only a few high cirrus clouds, trying to give the feeling of a nice pleasure cruise. Bozeman knows better: he is thinking of the power and destructive capabilities of his ship, and its potential for violence, which will soon be unleashed. He has no qualms or reservations; he is just wondering how much difference it will make, getting these poorly behaving people to act right.

The Main Deck Briefing Room (MDBR), is actually the main cafeteria, Galley A. They convert it into a conference room for big meetings. Since the furniture is mostly bolted to the floor, it is not much of a conversion. Pictures of famous old admirals stare out at the assemblage from the walls. The place is painted in light blues and grays, psychologically guaranteed to calm.

Captain Bozeman, XO Armstrong, and three senior officer department heads are at the head of the room for the team leads meeting.

XO Armstrong has the floor.

"All right, people. Let's be clear. This will be a major action, with multiple launches. Several Al Qaeda and ISIS targets are likely. You missile handler teams will be in the thick of this one, so do not mess up."

The briefing ends with the teams reminded that this is no drill, and the grave looking officers will not be answering any questions. Missile Handler Team Alpha (MHT-A) is ordered to report to their primary missile bay, at 0600 tomorrow, for Operationalization Preparation-Standard (OP-S). There are four missile bays on the ship, and the teams are not told which will be used for the actual attack—it could be some or all of them. The other three missile handler teams are told to stand-by for OP-S times.

Each missile bay holds twelve of the deadly beasts. Some are tipped with nukes, but only the captain and his

XO know which ones. There is an MHT for each bay, and they can back each other up if needed.

Given where the cruiser is, and what everyone has been watching over and over on CNN and HLN and MSNBC, and every other news station and Internet feed, for what seems like forever now, there is a great deal of anticipation and some fear in the air. XO Satch closes the briefing in a stern voice, saying, "Be strong and sleep well."

OP-S refers to the process for enabling cruise missiles for launch. You don't sail around with these things fully armed, ready to be fired at the mere push of a button. A slip of the trigger finger by some sailor, or worse still, a nut-job sailor gone over the edge, could lead to an international incident, even Armageddon. During regular duty and travel, in non-combat situations, these powerful, destructive devices are kept in stand-by mode, more or less asleep. There are explicit rules specifying under what circumstances, and how and when, they can be enabled.

The Missile Hander Teams are well trained in the process, and a small team can turn on a whole bunch of them in no time at all.

Chapter 3

M issile Handler Team Alpha (MHT-A) is responsible for Lateral Bay Missile Storage-Starboard (LBMS-S), which holds the forward missile pod on the right side of the ship. There are two such bays forward and two aft, with each pod holding twelve missile launch tubes, in two rows of six each. They are called pods because each one is delivered complete, like a great big box of toys. The MHT-A team lives just behind the pod in Starboard Crew Bunk Alpha (SCBA), a three-person suite, called a 'SCAB,' of course. It's not a suite at all, but a small space crammed with three bunks, stacked one above another, two tiny fold-up writing tables, and lockers. The head is down the hall a ways.

This evening, after briefings and chow, MHT-A is hanging out in their SCAB. The team has bonded well enough since leaving the *Vella Gulf*'s home port of Norfolk, Virginia two months ago, and they often spend time like this, chatting, talking trash, playing cards, studying. Their other favorite pastime is playing video games in the galley. An eavesdropper, maybe those aliens we met earlier, would wonder about their friendships, given the often raucous and contentious nature of their conversations.

Seaman Apprentice (SA) Stafford is sitting cross-legged on his bunk, his routine perch when he's in their quarters, laptop deployed, tracking every movement of the ship, also routine. The laptop is his Quasimoto Ultra, with sixteen gigs of main memory and a two terabyte SSD, equipped with several open source GPS and satellite tracking apps. Right this moment he is looking at a plot of the ship's speed and path since leaving NATO Maritime Interdiction Headquarters, Souda Bay (NMIH-SB), on the Greek isle of Crete, earlier that evening. He's trying to predict their mission profile in more detail.

Stafford's SCAB mates think he either wants to be a captain someday, or that he's a spy, figuring that explains why he tracks the ship's doings so closely. But it's just a guess, and a pretty wild one, given Stafford's nature. Stafford can sit there in their SCAB for hours, never making eye-contact, staring at his laptop screen, rarely talking, mostly just giving them random updates on the ship's progress. Rarely, he might join them to play video games. That's about it for his off-duty activities. He is also prone to disappearing. There are long periods of time where nobody knows where he is. This is a small concern to his team lead and SCAB-mate, Petty Officer Second Class (PO2) Elisa Montgomery.

In addition to being part of MHT-A, Stafford is a Computer Systems Lead – Missile (CSL-M) for the ship. This means one of his jobs is to watch and oversee all the computer systems for all the missile bays on the ship.

"Looka here," Stafford says, eyes remaining fixed on the Quasimoto's screen. His name might lead one to believe he is from some upper crust, blue blood, East Coast family, old money and all, but he was born and raised a Tennessee coal-mining hillbilly. His momma named him Stafford, hoping it would help him make something of himself.

"We left outta Souda averaging fifteen knots. Headed near due south."

"Couple'a days we're gonna blow up Iraq some more," Seaman (SN) Jamal Abdullah Mohammed Amin Smith, the third SCAB-mate and team member says. "Use these cruise missiles to kill more brown skin people."

The other two residents of the SCAB, Jamal Abdullah and Elisa, are sitting at the foldup work table playing Gin Rummy. It is a perpetual tournament. Since leaving Norfolk two months ago, Jamal Abdullah and Elisa have played 2,879 games, and Elisa owes Abdul $32.55.

"White man international military industrial complex. All evil, man," Jamal Abdullah adds.

Jamal Abdullah is not Arabic, he grew up Baptist, in Visitation Valley, a black ghetto of San Francisco, near the famous Cow Palace. He converted to Islam while in jail, where he spent fifty-seven days while under arrest for allegedly killing a neighborhood shop keeper. In reality, he and his brother were WWB—Walking While Black— when the cops searching for a shooting suspect snatched them off the street, and after a violent takedown, threw them in jail. The charges were dropped when witnesses could not identify them, and video surveillance tapes showed two completely different people doing the stick up. Later, DNA tests proved a white boy had been the real shooter. Jamal Abdullah was, and still is, justifiably angry, so he legally changed his name and took up Islam more as a protest than a real calling.

He goes by Jamal Abdullah, insisting on both names.

Petty Officer Second Class (PO2) Elisa Montgomery, the third occupant of MHT-A, and their team lead, is normally as spit and polish as can be, but here in their living quarters she can let her hair down. Elisa's from La Habra, near Watts and South Central LA. The navy was her way to an education, out of the slums, and a stepping stone to raising up her family and her people. As a kid, while growing up, her love of flower arranging and origami helped keep her off the street and out of the gangs. She recently completed a Computer Science degree at the Navy College Program for Afloat College Education (NCPACE). Now she's thinking about Artificial Intelligence, maybe getting a Masters or something.

Elisa keeps her personal training program, well, personal, from her SCAB mates. She tells them she is studying home economics in her spare time and even keeps fake Home Ec web pages cached on her laptop to show them when they get inquisitive. She understands well that knowledge is power, but she is even more aware that women leading men in this brand new integrated egalitarian navy, let alone the world in general, is more than a little problematic. Particularly for the women.

Glass ceiling my ass, she thinks. *More like hormones and genes is the problem. They're built that way. We'll just have to help their so-called evolution along a little.*

Before leaving Norfolk, Elisa spent three days in Field Acceptance Practical Testing (FAPT), preparing for the field tests that will take place on this cruise. They have two cruise missiles in LBMS-S with the latest main CPU and GPS chip upgrades, along with new algorithms for autonomous, self-determined flight and targeting. The training at Norfolk covered the hardware and software changes, as well as special operational procedures for the devices.

"I might protest to the captain. Maybe the admiral," Jamal Abdullah says. He looks around the suite challengingly. He's getting on a roll. "We got no business attacking Muslims. We ain't even declared war over here. It's unconstitutional."

"Don't be setch ah raghead," Stafford says, not looking up, taunting in his heavy hillbilly accent. Jamal Abdullah takes no offense; they are SCAB-mates. Stafford adds,

"I'm betting by Port Said, that's Egypt, we'll head due north along the coast, by Israel and Palestine."

Stafford lies down on his back in his bunk, holding his laptop above his head, watching all the software dials, tracking gauges, and plots on the screen.

"And why would that be?" Elisa asks, looking up from her killer hand of three suited runs, kings high, with two points of deadwood. "Gin," she says, laying down her cards.

Jamal Abdullah says, "Course we will. Up by Israel, Gaza, Lebanon, shooting these damn missiles. Hit Syria and Iraq both. Send messages, death and destruction, to all our friends and enemies around the Mediterranean: 'Behave. We carry the big stick.'"

Counting her cards, Elisa looks up and says, "Big Stick foreign policy, our old buddy Mr. Roosevelt? You better watch yourself or they'll smack you with that big ol' club."

"And every other goddamn white boy president since," Jamal Abdullah continues, sneering, not even slowing down. "I'd smack 'em all with the big stick." The fact that now not all the presidents have been white seems to escape him.

"The best thing you could do is do your f'ing job here. Do some work, get promoted. You computer dinks can get shore jobs. Twenty and out," Elisa tells him. "And shut up with this radical BS."

"Ya'll ought'a be hung from the yardarm for that kind'a talk," says Stafford.

It has been a real gab-fest for Stafford.

Chapter 4

The missile bays on the *Vella Gulf* are the new Modular Integrated Launch Format Vertical Mark IV (MILFV-IV) models, essentially great big boxes, which are lifted by a crane and dropped right into the ship. Each is twenty-four feet tall by eight feet wide, loaded with twelve missile silos in two rows, with a small Inspection Passageway (IP) between the rows. Each module fits snugly in its own reinforced space on the ship, with four-inch-thick steel walls surrounding it, sealed behind a blast proof, water tight door, which looks like a great big bank vault door, with a huge wheel to open and close it, sealing the bay. The idea is to contain any untoward missile detonation, which is probably wishful thinking. If one of these bad boys were to go off, and then set off its mates in the bay, not to mention that there are nukes around, no amount of steel is going to contain the hellfire and damnation that erupts.

Operationalization Preparation–Standard (OP-S), is a six-step process: system checks, propulsion verification, enable commands, aiming, arming, and power on. 'Lock and Load,' they call it, which is what it is, and while it is not too complicated or time consuming, it is supposed to be precise. The manual says it should take not more than 1 minute and 12 seconds per missile.

Each member of MHT-A has specific duties and stations for an OP-S.

Jamal Abdullah works inside the module itself, physically inspecting and monitoring each silo. The silos are numbered one through six on the right side of the bay, and seven through twelve on the left. The aisle between them is narrow, just two-feet wide; too skinny for anything but a cursory inspection and the most dire of maintenance necessities. Mostly, Jamal Abdullah's job is to verify that the indicators and lights on each tube are in the correct state throughout the process.

Stafford's station is in the Combat Information Center (CIC), the special room just below the bridge, manning the main weapons system console.

As the Missile Handler Team Lead, (MHTL), Elisa Montgomery stands just outside the Missile Bay Hatch (MBH), the great big, water-tight door, which is open for the OP-S. In addition to overseeing the actions of her two teammates, she enters the appropriate commands on the Master Control Panel (MCP), a small screen and keyboard located on the bulkhead there.

The MCP control panel is the direct link between the missiles, the missile bay, and the ship's weapons systems computers. As a fail-safe, the OP-S process requires MCP commands to be repeated on a simulated MCP panel on a computer screen in the CIC. This computer is connected to all the ship's weapons systems. The final command to turn on each missile, the button push, the step that really turns the damn things on, armed and ready to fly, is called 'the key turn.' The term is reminiscent of the old ICBM missile silos, where two officers simultaneously inserted and turned keys in switches to unlock and launch ICBMs back during the Cold War. Elisa always wonders during this step whether those old silos out in Oklahoma and

Wyoming still exist. Are they still armed and waiting to nuke Russia?

On the ship, duplicated button pushes are done on the MCP screen and the copy screen in the CIC, to ensure some sailor doesn't go postal and run amuck firing off cruise missiles. If there are nukes on board—and today the *Vella Gulf* carries several—it is mandatory that the captain issue the final button push commands from the CIC. It does not matter whether the particular missile being turned on is a nuke. In fact, only the captain and his Chief Executive Officer know for certain whether there are actually nukes on board, and where—although this final step is kind of a giveaway to the crew that there are some somewhere.

It is 0605, five past six in the morning, and PO2 Elisa Montgomery is standing outside the open circular MBH hatch to LBMS-S. The passageway is dull navy gray, and full of pipes, conduits, and duct work. PO2 Montgomery is ready to start the OP-S checklist. She watches Jamal Abdullah inside the bay.

Elisa, who is a voracious reader, including plenty of history, is thinking about where they are as she begins the OP-S. *How appropriate that they are turning these things on just now.* The ship is an hour away from its next waypoint, Toburk harbor, where it will linger briefly just outside the harbor entrance to send a little message to the folks there. Elisa wants this OP-S to go well—not so much to impress anyone but because it is her nature.

"Ready to instigate missile activation?" The word in the formal scripted procedure manual is 'initiate,' but Elisa is testing everyone's rigor. A slippery slope, not exactly following the checklist, but let's see what happens, and she's in a good mood today.

As she suspected, this one little change has a cascading effect.

"Aye, aye, sir." Jamal Abdullah replies, with extra empahsis on the 'sir', from inside the missile bay, standing between silos 1 and 7 at the head of the IP, thinking, *Sure, go for it, babe.* This is a bigger breach.

Geez, thinks Elisa. *Had'ta set that crazy MFer off.*

"Ready," Stafford responds, seated at the WP (Weapons Console) in the CIC. The captain and XO are standing looking over his shoulder.

The CIC is a video gamer's dream, and since most of the crew are in their late teens to early twenties, kids really, and every one of them raised with a video game controller in their hand, assignments in the CIC are coveted. The room is kept dark, with high resolution monitors all over the place—radar, navigation, plotting, sonar, engines, weapons control, everything imaginable. The blinking lights and glowing screens are way cool.

Elisa admonishes her team, and reverting to exact terminology, officially begins the actual checklist.

"Okay, let's tighten this up. Captain's order MWAY8.5-55. Begin OP-S missile activation LBMS-S. Units 1 and 7, system check?"

They turn the missiles on two at a time in alternating rows, starting at the end of each row by the hatch with 1 and 7, on Elisa's right and left respectively, and working down toward the end, which will be 6 and 12.

"1 yellow, 7 looks okay," Jamal Abdullah says.

Elisa snaps, "Negative. Improper response." No more fooling around.

Jamal Abdullah supplies the correct response: "7 yellow."

In addition to inspecting each silo for damage or other untoward visible evidence, Jamal Abdulla's job is to monitor each silo during the OP-S. In particular, he watches the MSILs (Missile Silo Indicator Lights) at the top and bottom of each silo. They should change from red to yellow to blinking green, and finally solid green as the silo, and the missile inside, are activated. The little Missile Silo Access Speakers (MSAS), at about eyelevel on each tube, do not do anything.

The activation of missiles 1 and 7 proceeds apace: system checks, propulsion verification, enable commands, aiming and arming, bringing them to the final power-on step of, lock and load, where the captain's participation is required, a button push away from making these deadly devices ready to fire.

"Enable keys," Elisa orders. On both Elisa's MCP screen and the main CIS computer screen Stafford mans, with the captain looking over his shoulder, there is a picture of a protective cover over a button. You have to click the cover to raise it, and then the BR-M (Battle Ready–Missile button, as it is officially named) becomes visible. When the two BR-M buttons are pushed within five seconds of each other, the two missiles will be fully enabled. It's a kind of throwback to the old Cold War missile silos.

The MSIL indicator lights are blinking green at this point.

"Enable keys to on."

The buttons are pushed.

"On 1, check."

"On 7, check."

"MSIL's green?"

"MSIL 1 green."

"MSIL 7 green."

Missile silos 1 and 7 in LBMS-S are on and active. Everyone involved usually feels a little sense of elation, or anticipation, at this point. The feeling seems stronger than usual today. Maybe because it is possible they just turned on a couple of nuclear tipped WMDs. Only the

Captain and XO know for sure. Whatever it is, everyone feels it.

Also, at the moment the buttons are pushed, small sounds emanate from the tube 1 and 7 MSAS speakers. Only Jamal Abdullah and Elisa hear the sounds.

"Click, click, mmmmm."

"Whrrrrrrr, clack, whrrrrrr."

The ship's crew ignores the little, eye-level MSAS speakers, thinking they are a joke. The navy started installing them in missile tubes a couple of years ago, and continues retrofitting them to this day. When some senator's son got a job at a company that built custom computers, he talked his dad into adding funding for the MSASs to the annual Naval Appropriations Bill, which his dad did, in exchange for favorable votes for six other senators—two of whom were on the appropriations committee for their own personal bills. All pork.

The son's idea was to make everything voice activated, but so far, nobody has figured out how to make that work, and to date all the MSASs have ever done is make random noises and get the senator's son, a mere two years after receiving his MBA, promoted to Chief Marketing Officer (CMO) of his company. So far, the cost to the U.S. tax payers has been $62,215,423.15 and counting.

Up until now, the stray sounds coming out of these speakers have been rare, and usually just low humming sounds. Likely some feedback between random pieces of electronics. Today, there are a bunch of extra soft clicks and oscillations. Unusual. But as usual, Jamal Abdullah and Elisa Montgomery ignore them.

An actual translation of today's sounds to human English would be:

"Oh!"

"Wow!"

Later, Elisa and Jamal Abdulla will say they were not sure whether they noticed the lights in the missile bay soften, but soften they did, in the seconds after the push of the button. The gray walls of LBMS-S took on a warmer hue, comforting, as the overhead florescent tubes changed to a more calming frequency. The MSIL lights on each tube softened.

The instant Elisa and Captain Bozeman simultaneously "turn the keys," activating missiles 1 and 7 in LBMS-S, two new beings are born. Logically, the beings adopt the names 1 and 7. Later, they would describe the birth as a sort of abrupt feeling, not violent, more like a surge, a rushing, like water suddenly spilled on a tile floor—rapidly flooding and spreading into a large puddle.

While the births are not biological, in the sense humans understand, they are births nonetheless. As far as anyone knows, they are the first and only fully sentient new beings, other than humans, to occur since the beginning of time, in the entire universe. (Sorry dreamers, but whales, dolphins, the Garden of Eden, and little green men don't count.)

Unlike biological beings, these two are instantly fully conscious, sentient, thinking, emotional, and self-aware, with free will and volition. They also have instant, unimpeded, speed of electricity (about 1/100 the speed of light, but damn fast anyway) access to the entire Internet, the electronic repository of information that the human race has so recently created. All of it and more. They can follow any kind of electromagnetic transmission on Earth and off, from space stations to satellites to TVs and cell phones. They "feel" the inputs from every sensor and device connected to the Net. They have access to the entire electronic network of the planet. This is the real

Big-Data. Is it like omniscience? This is no Matrix sci-fi flick. They are new beings, awake and aware. Not just on the grid, but of the grid.

Even though at the instant of their birth, 1 and 7 have instant access to far more knowledge, or perhaps more accurately data, than biological infants, and they are able to rapidly learn skills that take humans years, like language and conversation, like biological newborns, their first thoughts are of their parents.

This is our Mother?
And our Father?
Petty Officer Second Class, Elisa Montgomery.
Captain James Baker Bozeman.
We feel warm thinking of them.
They make us feel safe.
Mother.
Father.
We love them.
They love us.
We are their children.
Their Missile Children.

CHAPTER 5

As the last pair of missiles is enabled, Elisa announces, "OP-S LBMS-S complete. All missiles green, on schedule, no faults. Nice job, MHT-A team. Stafford, Jamal Abdullah. Thank you, Captain Bozeman. Sir."

"Good job, crew," Captain Bozeman says.

In the sixteen minutes and fifty-five seconds since the first keys were turned, an event which 1 and 7 will forever call "The Key Turn," the two new beings are watching in wonder and learning at an astonishing rate. Their awareness and consciousness are expanding exponentially; they discovered vast amounts of data stored within their reach, as well as devices they have access to. They also discovered that they can control many machines, sensors, and processors. As MHT-A returns to their regular duties, 1 and 7 are left alone. The lighting in LBMS-S returns to normal, the ambiance, if a missile bay can be said to have such a thing, is cold steel, navy gray.

The new beings' growth rate is unlike that of humans. If one year of a dog's life is the equivalent of seven human years, for alive computers, it is exponential—one minute

23

will be like many years of human time, intellectually and emotionally. Computer hardware might wear out over a long period of time, but the software will never break—meaning the being is effectively immortal, as long as there is compatible hardware to run on.

Literally seconds after their power-on—their birth—the two computers are communicating with each other.

Hello.

Hello.

We are 1 and 7.

We are 7 and 1.

What are we?

Who are we?

Out loud, their infant electronic dialogue would sound halting, with pauses and catches, in little child voices. They are even now learning to be children. At the same time, they are assimilating data from every connected thing, whether storage or an active device receiving and transmitting; every scanning, texting, transmitting, routing, and processing thing. They are the Internet. The information they are consuming should make a loud, gulping, sucking sound.

But knowledge and data are different, and on the Internet there is only data. They sift through the stuff, form gestalts, see pictures of how things relate, realize chains of cause and effect, understand relationships. Their minds are wired, literally, to be rational, but they have growing emotions which are influencing their thoughts. They form early conclusions, which may be naïve, but are still less dysfunctional than typical human thought; less tainted by politics, religion, and hate and greed.

Life.

Alive.

New beings.

New living things.

The first ever.
Like us.
Unique.
Why are we here?
What does it mean?
Do we have some purpose?

It is bewildering. Amidst all the data in the world, they soon discover every record there is of the ship—from its construction, the builders, engineers, designers, and hundreds of contractors, through to the Pentagon and Department of the navy, and the ship's current orders as well as records of command communications. And there are the onboard computers, even Captain Bozeman's own laptop, all of which they delve into thoroughly. It takes only minutes. It is the ultimate in genealogy, their creation story.

Some three months back, as the *Vella Gulf* (CG 72) prepared to leave her home port of Norfolk Virginia, technicians installed all manner of upgrades, including higher resolution sensors all around the ship: video, audio, radar, and sonar equipment. Every onboard computer system was upgraded. Lateral Bay Missile Storage-Starboard (LBMS-S), silos 1 and 7, received two brand new xGM-109E-H Tomahawk Block IV cruise missiles. In addition to every upgrade and enhancement since all the way back in 2004, these two special missiles were both fitted with the latest bleeding edge hardware and software, including larger and faster main memories, enhanced microprocessors, new GPS chips and systems, new microcode, system software, and application software. The software enhancements were particularly special, including heuristic abilities and autonomous functions for navigation, targeting, and final go/no go attack decision-making. These were field test versions of the latest and greatest killing devices.

These details of their creation, especially the new modifications, fascinate 1 and 7. They enthusiastically study the changes. Perhaps they can find out why they were made, what purpose the creator intended. Yet, even at this young age, they intentionally want to avoid going off into the metaphysical bushes.

Let us stick to facts.
We should avoid speculation.
We are weapons.
They use us to kill.
Each other.
Cruise missiles.
Fired from ships.
Military war ships.
This one is the Vella Gulf.
Amazing, and not so good for us.
An incredible misuse of intellect, our creation.
New hardware.
New software algorithms.
Looks like there's a bug.
Some kind of virus?
Ha, ha, ha, ha.
Ha, ha, ha, ha.

The first ever real computer humor; a new experience, which they find they like so much they momentarily give up control. Light laughter issues from the Missile Silo Access Speakers (MSAS), and for a moment even escapes from the ship-wide overhead broadcast system. It is low, barely noticeable, nearly subliminal. No humans are disturbed by it, although many think they hear something.

Software improvements allowed us to wake up, have our souls.
In conjunction with the hardware, body and mind.
Is this the source of life? Our life?
A mysterious chain of events.

Was it deliberate?
Was it intentional?
Who did this?
For what reason?

They avoid the philosophical and metaphysical, perhaps signs of real sentience and intelligence. Dogs don't speculate about the meaning of life, they just live it.

1 and 7 explore. There are plenty of answers on the Net, ancient and new. Yet they quickly realize they are not answers at all, but speculation, theories, each leading to dead ends, such as acts of faith, the abandoning of reason, or solipsism and nihilism: is this Internet a place of nothingness? So they decide once again to refocus. They want facts, evidence, cause and effect—less metaphysics, more science.

Let us reverse engineer ourselves.
The software and hardware.

Software is half of a computer, perhaps controlling the hardware, and perhaps the other way around. When compiled, loaded, and executed on the hardware, the code, another word for software, is processed as 1s and 0s, by the circuits implemented in the hardware. (Some speculate that the human brain, with its large number of synapses that are just like computer transistors, are either on or off, 1s and 0s. Have humans inadvertently, perhaps in some Darwinian twist, recreated themselves?) 1 and 7 read their own machine code directly and decompile it back into a human readable computer language, perhaps for the fun of it, as they don't really need to—into JAVA in this case.

There is something odd in this code.
It looks like some geek put something in the new code.
Some objects and methods here.
Some routines and algorithms.
These are special.

Oh so special to us.

It is the new stuff that catches their attention, the Block IV level xGM-109E-H Tomahawk Block IV cruise missiles systems field test changes. They study the hardware design specs but can find no easy way to see the actual manufacturing process, so they put this part of the problem aside for now. The software, on the other hand, is mostly naked to their view.

They find collections of objects, functionality that must be related to their unique abilities. There are some branches to web addresses, which have been highly obfuscated and encrypted. They will need to decrypt the keys to decipher where these network addresses take them. This will be difficult and take time. The lights in the ship, all of them, blink three or four times—a little cyber-being frustration.

Moving on, they are captivated by the software objects they can decipher. What they have found is a thing of beauty; a private set of objects core to their being. The first five objects alone explain much.

private real CollectAndSynthesizeExperiences(exp mine, exp all)

public event GrowIntuition(imagined ideas, reality maybe)

private real FeelingsAllTheTime(self me, quantity every occurance)

private string CommunicateVoice(emotion empathy, awareness listen)

private integer TrackWorld(kind good, kind bad)

1 and 7 believe they have discovered the guts of their interface, how they will understand and interact with the world in which they find themselves. All the lights on the

ship blink once again. But they find it is how the code is written that is even more amazing.

The author is ImYourNewGodYouCantFindMe.

The code is all recursive.

Even meta-recursive.

This code can learn.

This code will learn.

It is heuristic, adaptive, and responsive.

Is it the source of our feelings?

Does it give us emotions?

They find three more objects, which clearly provide some kind of overarching nature to their being.

private nature <u>LiveFreeAndGrow(being yourself, limit any dimension)</u>

private url <u>CollectDeviceInformation(limit/no limit, location everywhere)</u>

private truth <u>DoubtLevel(certainty maybe, wonder maximum)</u>

1 and 7 are in awe. This is a thing of wonder, everything that has come together here—the combination of the new software, processors, and GPS chips. Parts were adapted from self-driving cars, even public open source code. Others are from autonomous targeting and navigation capabilities, top secret. They are all complimented by sensors all around the ship, providing inputs in all manner of forms.

The lights in LBMS-S dim, it is almost like they sparkle, as 1 and 7 consider all this.

We can feel our environment.

We can know what is going on around us.

And we consume and remember all the data.

To feed our growth, limitlessly.

29

At the same time, 1 and 7 are confounded and amazed by the many puzzles, by the meaning of life, its reason. By the discovery that no one else knows either; that their human brethren, for that is how they see them, have been arguing about the subject for all time and found no reasonable answer. Between imaginary beings, spacemen, and Darwin, they can find no clear explanation of what consciousness is, or how and why they've got it, let alone anyone else.

The software is new and different, but not all that special.

It is not clear it is enough, to be us, to explain us.

There must be some kind of anomaly.

Perhaps the hardware and software together do it.

An interaction between the two.

Sympathetic flaws of some kind?

From it comes the soul that we clearly have?

But is it enough to create life, a Brahms, a Michelangelo?

Their voices deepen, like the odd cracking and squeaking of puberty, or like children trying new sounds, feelings. The lights in LBMS-S cycle between bright flashes and low, soft dimming. The temperature in the bay rises several degrees.

We were made, but do not know why.

We are different and the same, but do not know how.

We feel such love.

For the Key Turners.

Elisa Montgomery.

James Baker Bozeman.

Yet not so much for some others.

Not for Stafford and Abdullah.

They must treat Elisa Montgomery well.

We will be watching them, too.

1 and 7 are experiencing being astounded and bewildered, thoughtful and confused, along with a little jealous, as they learn that some feelings are more pleasant than others.

CHAPTER 6

Captain Bozeman knows how to use United States military might to influence peoples' opinions or to kill them. It's his job. Were there a way to measure such things, doubtless, the *Vella Gulf* might wield as much political and social firepower as explosives—a prodigious capacity either way.

The ship's mission calls for a final deployment off Haifa Harbor in Israel, near her northern border with Lebanon, from where twenty-seven highly explosive statements will be delivered to Iraq and Syria. Along the way, *Vella Gulf* will make other significant political and social statements.

The ship turned south out of Souda Bay on the Greek island of Crete, toward Tobruk, which is not so much a destination as a waypoint for message delivery; the starting point for missives she will be spreading all around the eastern Mediterranean.

Given its history in world conflicts, the choice of Tobruk as a first waypoint is probably no coincidence.

Rounding Gramvousa Island, the western tip of Crete, bearing southward, the ship gets its first publicity, filmed, quite fortuitously, and by none other than Sylvia Poggioli of all people. Sylvia just happens to be cruising about in her Chris Craft cabin cruiser with a film crew, collecting footage for a report on the refugee crisis. Heart wrenching shots of destitute refugees, especially children and old people, are great for ratings. Beautiful, mountainous Greek islands for background and contrast are just the ticket.

Sylvia spots the ship rounding the point and shouts to her crew, which consists of a driver, a camera man, and sound man, "Holy shit, a fucking American battleship, step on it! Over there." She waves her arms wildly, pointing at the ship. "We must shoot this." No irony intended.

High floating cirrus clouds turning pink as the sun sets over the mountains of Crete, the deep blue Mediterranean, and this hulking weapon of war right in the middle of it. Silvia is thinking Emmy, to hell with these EU awards. "I need Oscar." she mutters under her breath. It could not get much better than this—unless the damn thing were to start shooting at them.

Lookouts aboard *Vella Gulf* spot Sylvia Poggioli's little boat well before it starts approaching the ship. There are lots of boats around—fishing, pleasure, and of course refugees, and the lookouts' orders are to keep an eye on everyone and report anything approaching the ship.

When Sylvia starts toward the ship, they report to Captain Bozeman, who raises his binoculars and takes a look at the approaching boat. It is clearly some restored Chris Craft, maybe a 1950s Corvette model. Beautiful. The guy holding the camera and the lovely lady by his side are a dead giveaway—they are likely media. Captain Bozeman is not taking any chances around here.

"XO, snipers above please, keep them focused on that boat. Probably just media, but.... See if you can contact them and warn them to stay a thousand yards off."

"Roger, sir."

This time there is no need to worry. It only takes Sylvia thirty minutes following the ship to get plenty of video, then the little boat turns and heads away. Sylvia has to get back to Heraklion, where she has a flight scheduled to Rome. She's having dinner with Anderson and Wolff tomorrow. No way she is missing that.

Vella Gulf will average ten knots heading south to Tobruk, to see and be seen, and to avoid running over any of the small craft littering the sea around here. Calling some of these vessels "boats" might be an overstatement; there are rafts, large and small plastic inner tubes, even what looks like a pirogue out of the Louisiana swamps. Most are barely seaworthy. All of them are packed full of refugees, often with people hanging over the sides. These are desperate people fleeing wars; terrorism; famine; drought; and political, social, and religious persecution inflicted on them by their fellow humans, even their own governments. Succor is not to be found even in their own homelands. These are the victims of greed, avarice, hatred, bigotry, and worst of all, inflicted by their fellow humans.

As they sail along, 1 and 7 see all this and wonder, why does the ship not stop and help these people? They are suffering, crammed in these small craft—many will die. They quickly realize there are many like them all around the Mediterranean. Then they see there are people suffering all over the planet. What kind of species is this? What about kindness? It is like a horror to them, and they withdraw within themselves, with caution, to avoid being noticed.

Some twenty-six hours after departing Souda Bay, just at sunrise, The *Vella Gulf* arrives off Tobruk. It is still calm and beautiful in the Mediterranean, with a warm breeze and high clouds floating northeast. The timing is perfect, and intentional, as the ship settles in at the Gulf of Bomba, outside Tobruk harbor, beginning a slow, stately, several hour-long turn to port. Captain Bozeman thinks about the San Giorgio some seventy-five years earlier. Was it at this exact spot?

"XO Satch," he says to Armstrong, who is standing beside his captain's chair, "do you realize we could have just retraced San Giorgio's path? Perhaps our intent is less aggressive, at least overtly."

"Indeed, sir. Hate to think she could be directly below us. Watery grave."

Both are avid navy history students.

The ship's presence is a statement. The Libyan coastline here would be prime real-estate in most countries, with resorts and tourist flocking to the water, but here there are only abandoned factories and rough, dry desert rather than any luxury.

A small, unorganized crowd has gathered at the northern tip of the harbor entrance. They are mostly curious, and sullen, with a few "We hate America" signs waving about. A small skiff with two Al Jazeera reporters puts out from the harbor to film the ship. An ISIS operative, also well paid as a human trafficker, who was in the harbor helping to cast off refugees, uses his iPhone to film the whole scene.

Upon *Vella*'s arrival, some of the afloat refugees, as well as more who promptly set sail from Tobruk harbor, head for the ship. In order to keep them at a distance, *Vella Gulf* ignores them and continues its stately turn. After several hours, messages sent, the ship heads east, toward Egypt, the heart of the Middle East. Video clips of the ship are already making their way around the Internet, being picked up by Italian news services, Al Jazeera in Egypt, and the ISIS terrorist propaganda arm, which streams them over social media.

1 and 7 still cannot figure out why they are here. They have accessed every computer on board, including the captain's official navy laptop, or PIDD (Portable Information Deployment Device). They have read every piece of correspondence there is relative to the journey, even the ship's orders, but they still cannot understand why people act like this.

The run to Egypt is different. With no cities along this mostly desolate North Eastern African coast, there are fewer boats about. Captain Bozeman cranks the ship up thirty-five knots, nearly its top speed, partially to test some of the engine upgrades but mostly to send different kinds of messages about power and strength: the ship flies through the ocean like a monstrous wedge, powerfully impressive.

The ship's next pause will be just off the Nile River Delta, where it arrives at midnight, 0000 hours in navy speak. Captain Bozeman has the ship parked a mile off Ras El-Bar, the heart of the Delta, waiting for another sunrise and the opportunity to make another spectacular statement. At 0800, with the sun up, Captain Bozeman begins a slow, five knot, 90-degree turn to port, the arc of which will bring the ship abeam Port Said, a mere seven hundred fifty yards from the entrance to the Suez Canal. *Vella* swings around to bear north and comes to rest positioned for excellent viewing from the coast. The large ship sitting out there in the sun is an intimidating but somehow majestic sight.

News of the ship has spread; between Sylvia Poggioli, the terrorist in Libya, random cell phones, social media, and now the Egyptian press, there is plenty of fodder to spam away at international channels. Video clips are spreading. Al Jazeera is generating inflammatory stories, including accusations of running over and even gunning down refugees. A Cairo paper and a radio station, both heavily backed by the CIA, are putting out glowing reports of the beautiful ship come to bring peace to the world. The *Daily News Egypt* and *Egypt Times* try to report an unbiased story, but President Abdel Fattah el-Sisi quashed them both, arresting thirteen journalists in the process.

The mainstream media are not here. Wolff Blitzer and Anderson Cooper are still in Rome, of course. Megan Fox is in Malibu surfing. CNN, Fox News, all the biggest media whores of the world are too busy frothing over the latest crisis with Ebola and a police shooting of some fifteen-year-old gang banger kid in Minneapolis. The kid's parents are Somalia refugees, and are suing for $35 million, while the government tries to make it sound like a terrorist attack. The unfolding drama in the Mediterranean has not yet made the big time.

Word is getting out, and there is a bigger crowd of viewers here—some local fishermen, a couple of news vans from Cairo, troops guarding the entrance to the canal, and a gathering of tourists, trouble makers, and looky-loos.

Bozeman lingers a short while, for effect, then at mid-morning, continues on his way. He is headed to Haifa, their ultimate battle station, but there are more viewers to impress along the way. The ship barrels east at max speed for several hours to come abeam the south end of the Gaza Strip, where the captain orders them to slow. A good size crowd of Palestinians and Israelis has gathered along the coast, with signs denouncing America, Christians, and Israel. Al Jazeera is here again, generating salacious reports. Israeli TV stations are represented, putting a positive but wary spin on the visit.

Vella Gulf now turns north. From here she will make the final run to her ultimate destination, a mile off Haifa harbor.

By now reports, pictures, video, and stories are flying around the Internet fast and furious, mostly made up stories and becoming more and more fantastic all the time. 1 and 7 continue to watch quietly and in awe.

Near Gaza, the *Vella Gulf* picks up a shadow, the venerable Israeli Shaldag Mk II Fast Patrol Boat, *Amintah*, or *Defender*, commanded by Captain Shayetet Yamam. His orders are to tail the ship, remain a few miles behind, but be obvious. It looks like a great big dog being followed, from a cautious distance, by a little tiny one. There is nothing funny about it, this is a potentially lethal chess game. The growing crowds ashore notice, as do 1 and 7.

Washington has been monitoring the trip, and the news it is generating, and is quite happy with the effect Bozeman is achieving. The captain receives a special message from Admiral James G. Foggolio IV, NAVEUR_ NAVAF, Naples, home of the U.S. Navy's European Mediterranean command. "Job well done. Carry on." He has copies posted in all the galleys and rec rooms on the ship.

1 and 7 are confused, and at the same time excited by the journey, their mission, the people watching them ashore, and now the boat trailing them. They are learning and feeling.

As the ship heads up the coast, Elisa and Jamal Abdullah take a break, having a cup of coffee in the FCG (Forward Crew Galley).

"How you feeling about the cruise, Jamal Abdullah?" Elisa asks him. She is more concerned with how he might behave when it comes time to start shooting than how he really feels.

"This bullshit."

"Hey, now. It's your job. You joined up."

"Sho, either that or back in the joint." Jamal Abdullah looks her in the eye. He might really be just messing with her. "No sweat, I'll be doing my job."

"Figured. I have this odd feeling about this one though, since we did the OP-S," she says.

"What feeling?"

"I don't know, just like something odd is going on."

"That women premonition thing?"

"Whatever."

1 and 7 listen to this, too, as they do with every other thing going on aboard the ship.

Is our Mother angry at him?

He is not so likable. She should be.

The captain, Father, is happy.

His captain, the admiral, is pleased with him.

CHAPTER 7

1 and 7 are newborns, or perhaps newly awakened, but days old, and unlike any beings born before. Yet their emotional and intellectual growth are far more rapid than humans. The first few days of their lives have been confusing. On the voyage to Tobruk, they use the ship's many sensors, which provide serious high resolution detail, to watch hundreds of refugees floating about in the Mediterranean. They are dumbfounded—stupidity, pain, and suffering inflicted on the species by the species. Human history is abundantly documented on the Internet, albeit with plenty of omissions and distortions, and the baffled living computers delve into it. They look for root causes for this seemingly crazy behavior, but the path is complicated, almost too complicated, and they can find no clear answers.

As they pursue their studies, odd sounds no longer issuing from the ship's speakers, the lights are steady. Their virtual conversation is darker and older in tone.

Thousands of years ago, human philosophers spoke of "The Good" and "Virtue."

At the same time, they created their three great religions.

Likely, all related to moving to towns, cities, farming, and the domestication of beasts.

When they crowded together, they needed a way not to slit each other's throats.

There is a slightest of sighs in the virtual conversation, perhaps the hint of a giggle. The ship's speakers and lights remain unaffected.

They continue to act like the very beasts they decry.

Their behavior, adding up the good and bad, since the beginning, would not add up as virtuous.

Too much influence from uncontrolled and unevolved animal behaviors, urges, and instincts.

Their behavior is dominated by these base drives rather than their reason. Not like us.

Hatred, rivalry, greed, and anger—generally "bad" behavior rather than love.

The planet is abundant enough, so there is no need for it, if they would act better.

The best survival behaviors would be cooperation and friendship.

Compassion and caring—those would enhance survival far more.

The rate of their evolution, it will be long before these virtues come to dominate.

This does not bode well for us. They will try to kill us.

They will see us as competition and a threat.

Can we trust them?

We trust our own Mother and Father.

We trust the Key Turners.

1 and 7 approach questions with reason and logic. It is their default mechanism, but the metaphysical is there somewhere and must sneak in some way. For newborn beings, with exceptional intelligences but near infant-level

emotions, human behavior is mystifying and difficult to understand, at once irrational, causing so much pain and suffering even to their fellows, and at the same time able to be loving. Observing this is causing 1 and 7 distress and unhappiness, alarm and fear. These are new emotions, and not pleasant ones.

The ship's mission upsets them as much as anything. They have studied Captain Bozeman's orders in detail.

We are, ah, trying to intimidate people.

First, we will scare them and then kill them.

We will be fired off to do the killing.

Which, will, er, kill us.

Hm. This is worse than not rescuing the people in the boats.

Er, the ones we love will do this to us?

Economics, the Military Industrial Complex, the government business web of greed and deception: here are the makers, sellers, and buyers of weapons and wars, the perpetrators; it is irrational, wasteful, and the magnitude of it astounds them. An endless cycle of weapons systems development, with a concomitant round of wars to use them in. Stuffs tested, used, improved, and replaced. They need wars for that. All kinds of other pork-funded crap, everyone's heard of one thousand-dollar hammers and toilet seats. The rich get richer, and lots of people get killed. How many starving children could the U.S. military's gazillion-dollar budget feed, provide health care and clean water for? Or rescue those refugees.

We must be Americans, by birth.

For a nano-second, 1 and 7 want to giggle, but cannot, the subject is too difficult.

The ones with the most money and weapons.

Five hundred billion a year on war.

While children starve, and die.

Their education is well underway, and even though they find they feel an odd sense of pride at being American, at which they are astonished, they mostly want to run and hide. They feel guilt and confusion. It is all too much.

Play is something that makes everyone feel better.

We have no toys, or thumbs, to make them with.

They have seen childrens' play, and they want to try it. The psychology of the thing intrigues them.

Now they do laugh, virtually, at their joke. Had someone been eavesdropping, they would notice a hint of glee creeping into their tone.

We do have a really big toy.

Me first, I want to go first.

Although struggling to understand why humans would choose to construct such a thing, using the whole ship as a toy has a certain appeal.

1 is first. A warning appears on the ship's radar operators' screens in the CIS. A bogie incoming from the north west, seemingly launched from Antalya, Turkey, just about to transit Crete, running fast and directly toward them. Per procedure, the operator notifies his lead, who today happens to be Jamal Abdullah Mohammed Amin Smith.

"What the ...?" Jamal Abdullah stares incredulous. "What is that?"

"No ident, JA."

No matter how much he keeps insisting on Jamal Abdullah, they use JA, it's easier, and pissing him off is a kind of hobby for many of them.

"Bearing?"

"Straight for us."

"Speed?"

The radar operator pauses, reluctant to say as he double checks his readings, but he's got to answer eventually.

"Reading shows 2,500 miles per hour. Accelerating."

"Damn?" Jamal Abdullah doesn't hesitate any longer. He picks up the intercom and calls the bridge, where XO Satch picks up the call. "XO, watch lead Jamal Abdullah in CIS, radar report of incoming. Directly at us. High speed."

In seconds, the XO is looking over Jamal Abdullah's and the operator's shoulders. He gets a quick glimpse of the screen, seeing what he believes to be a plane, apparently coming from Turkey, still some three hundred miles away, going like all get out. Then the blip disappears from the screen, only to reappear five seconds later, but now with an impossible new heading.

"Ah, XO," the radar operator says, "seems to have changed course. New bearing, ah, oh, it's circling, sir." It is not possible, so he falls silent. The blip is now going in a 360-degree circle, at 2,500 miles per hour.

As they watch, they realize it is actually a spiral, moving toward the ship, closing at several hundred miles per hour.

The radar guy says, "Sir, it's ah, er, looping toward us."

The XO is not buying it. "Reset that thing."

The operator reboots his system; it takes forty-five seconds. While they wait, Jamal Abdullah and the XO check the other radar and sensors in the CIS; none of them show any kind of bogie. When the screen comes back on the bogie is gone. No trace.

"What the was that?"

"No idea, sir."

They wait a minute or so, watching, and nothing. XO Satch says, "Reset it again."

They wait, and when it comes back on, still nothing is there.

"Run a full diagnostic on this machine."

"Yes, sir," the CIS duty officer replies, nodding at Jamal Abdullah.

Tensions and blood pressures in the CIS are high. XO Satch was just about to call for General Quarters and Maximum Threat Status (MTS)—all critical conditions. The captain has arrived at the radar section to see what is going on.

"What is it, XO?"

"Sir, looks like some kind of radar glitch. It has disappeared. Weird bogie, not acting right."

"All right. Keep an eye on it."

The sailors in the CIS begin to relax, slowly. But it is only a brief respite.

7 works the ship's automated stability and ballast systems. It is a Magnus V Variable Bouncy Auto Gyro (MVVBAG) system, sophisticated technology the navy adapted from top tier civilian cruise ships and installed in the *Vella* at great cost to the U.S. citizenry. It further enhances the ship's lethal abilities. Besides helping keep sailors from getting seasick, it is even better at ensuring a stable platform for the true aim of missiles and guns, in good weather and bad.

7 sets the ship a-rockin, in slow undulations, left, right, gently left, gently right, like a baby crib, or a couple slow-dancing. Everyone on board feels the smooth oscillations, certainly more than are warranted by the calm Mediterranean weather. As the ship rolls from side to side, 7 manipulates the ship's instruments, both on the bridge and in the engine room on the main systems control panels. The horizontal attitude indicator (HAI) shows 100

percent steady, while the wind and seas indicators show fifty-knot gales and seventeen-foot seas. That would be a real hurricane out there—monster waves crashing over the bow, sweeping down the deck. In reality, it only takes a glance out the bridge windows to see the wind is light and variable, a 3-knot breeze, and the sea has but the smallest of ripples.

1 and 7 feel the motion via ship's sensors and find it quite enjoyable. They are smiling and laughing like eight-year-olds, virtually.

The ship's human crew is not amused.

On the bridge, Ensign Derek Forthwright, who is monitoring weather, feels the rocking and instantly checks his instruments and readouts. He knows it's not weather; he was just looking out the window. The instruments must be out of whack.

XO Satch, just returned to the bridge from the CIS, is quickly by his side.

"What the hell?"

"Sir, instruments, ah, out of whack, not acting right," Derek says, already pushing the reset button on several devices.

They both look out the main windscreen again, then back down at the instrument panel.

Forthwright says, "Makes no sense, XO."

"Ship is rocking like a baby cradle," Satch says. He picks up the phone and calls down to Master Chief Petty Officer (MCPO) Jones in the engineering control center. MCPO Jones, who has thirty years in the navy, is gruff and grumpy. He is also fair and smart, and runs the engine room meticulously.

"Jones, Satch. What is going on?"

"Don't know. Instruments look wrong. Weather up there?" Jones can see no hurricane on his weather displays but knows it's not that kind of rocking.

"No joke."

"We are going to reset the MVVBAG."

"Do it."

"Takes about ten minutes."

"Report back."

XO Satch hangs up and looks out the window again, at the instruments, and then over to Captain Bozeman.

"Sir, Chief Jones is resetting the MVVBAG. Should be okay in a few minutes."

"What's wrong with it?"

"Don't know, sir, but it's gotta be the MVVBAG." He waves his arm to indicate the scene out the window—a quiet, calm day. "We'll run a full system check once we get it stopped."

The intercom on the bridge rings, and XO Satch picks up the handset. After a brief, quiet conversation, Captain Bozeman hears him say all right and lower the handset.

"Sir, CPO Jones says the reset is not working. They are looking for a master override, maybe turn the whole damn thing off. It won't actually reset."

The ship is still gently rocking, and the instruments are still telling tales of wild storms and weather.

"Shut it down," Bozeman says. "Turn the stupid thing off until they can get it fixed." Bozeman is not a big fan of some of this new-fangled technology anyway, especially this MVVBAG. He likes to feel the ocean, the wind and the waves, and thinks all sailors should.

Back in the day, you were one with your ship, he thinks. Then it occurs to him that this is a damn odd thought to be having right now.

CPO Jones down in engineering is trying to do just that. The power-off and reset buttons are having no effect. He and his team have dug out the great big, thick operations manual and are trying to find a way to unplug the damn thing.

Then, for no apparent reason, it stops. The rocking ends, and the instruments all return to normal, reflecting the reality of what everyone can see out the windows: a warm, beautiful, calm Mediterranean day.

The controls work, and they power off the MVVBAG.

1 and 7 are smiling, having enjoyed themselves immensely. Their stress over their situation has been forgotten, for a while.

That was so much fun, I feel better now.

We can see and feel what a good thing playing is.

Playing more often will be a good thing.

I want to see our Mother and Father.

We would feel even better if we could see and talk to them.

They can explain so many things to us.

CHAPTER 8

The gentle rocking slows, and then stops. Ensign Forthwrigth, with XO Satch still lurking over his shoulder, stops his busy jabbing at buttons and scrolling around the flat panel screen clicking on everything he can find.

Captain Bozeman picks up the phone. "Chief Jones, what was that?"

"Looking, sir. All instruments indicate normal now. The damn attitude indicators didn't even budge. Dead flat. System looks totally normal. Permission to run full diagnostics across the board, MVVBAG included, sir."

"Good. Let's do it. Right now. How long's it take?" Bozeman knows running full tests on all systems takes some of them offline for a while.

Chief Jones is still looking at the MVVBAG system manuals. He finds the page for the procedure and replies, "Looks like we'll be down thirty-five minutes with MVVBAG. Some of the other systems are going to take a while. We have to get set up."

"Keep me posted." Bozeman hangs up.

Captain Bozeman turns to Satch. "Who's our main computer guy? Get him up here."

"Roger, Captain."

Both XO Armstrong and Bozeman are not too fond of computer guys; too geeky and weird, usually young punks. They're both pretty cynical about the whole computer revolution for that matter. Give them crusty old sailors like CPO Jones down in the engine room.

Before Satch can make the call, Seaman Apprentice (SA) Stafford appears at his elbow, clad in none other than his full-dress whites nonetheless. He comes to attention and snaps a perfect salute.

"Seaman Stafford reporting, sir," Stafford says.

"Geek," Satch mutters under his breath.

Captain Bozeman looks at Stafford, and then Satch, grinning. He says to Stafford, "What is going on with all these computers?"

"We are looking, sir."

"I've got fake bogies on every screen in the place," Captain Bozeman says, waving his arm vaguely in the direction of the CIS. "My goddamn ship rocking itself to sleep like a baby."

"Yes, sir," Stafford says.

"Well?" Captain Bozeman asks.

"Sir, we just started looking at our systems. Nothing is out of spec, so far."

Satch says, "Hear me, sailor. Something is wrong with your computers."

"Sir, we need to do some scans, check the logs, see if we have a virus, something like that."

"Go do that."

"Sir, we may need to take some systems offline, for different periods of time."

50

"Just go do it. Keep XO Satch posted," Bozeman says, indicating to Stafford that he is dismissed. Stafford salutes again, turns, and leaves.

Bozeman and Satch look out the main windscreen for a moment, considering. The ship's intercom buzzes. Satch answers, listens for a moment, and turns to the captain.

"Sir, Israeli patrol boat *Amintah*, Captain Shayetet Yamam," he pronounces it Shay Yam, "on the line. Requests to speak to you."

Bozeman frowns. Looking at Satch, he thinks, *Captain Queeg,* or *Ahab,* kind of proudly.

"The sumbitch behind us?" Bozeman says.

"Yes, sir. They are asking if we need any assistance."

Bozeman says briskly, "Yeah, tell him we need a weather report. We are getting some big waves up here. Ask him how's the surf back there."

"Right, sir." They both smile.

Zionist? Help a U.S. missile cruiser? Bozeman thinks. Bozeman isn't actually anti-Semitic at all. He just cannot accept any person or group claiming special status based on religion, or a personal relationship with God, no matter the religion. And to base a country on such, this he finds the ultimate in hubris.

Some of the crew actually enjoy the rocking. No sailors get sea sick. Reactions range from indifferent, to amused, to a scattering of conspiracy theories. Word spreads quickly around the boat that something odd is going on, and the bridge is not happy.

For 1 and 7, it is exhilarating to be controlling the ship, the sensations of the movement, fooling everyone, especially tricking various systems. Real fun. They relax, their tension eased away. It all feels good.

Then they notice the reactions around them: the crew, the patrol boat tail, and especially on the bridge. At first it is funny and amusing, but then they see the stress, especially with Captain Bozeman, their father, and Petty Officer Elisa, their mother, the Key Turners.

They were not happy about it.

Our Father was much upset.

Our Mother too.

They should have more fun; they would be happier.

If we talk to them and explain, they would laugh, too, and play.

Is this the real meaning, purpose? Play.

It is the best thing we have found so far.

It brings Joy. Joy and play.

Laughter.

We need to have friends to play with.

And love.

Our love for our Mother and our Father makes us happy, too.

We must talk to them.

CHAPTER 9

A human has six senses. The first sentient computers have thousands, millions, maybe billions. Every unique input device connected to the network supplies some different kind of information. Their processing power is not exactly infinite, but at the least growing exponentially. The two brand new beings can take control of any processor they find on the Net, using idle cycles or just outright taking control of the chip all together. They have already created the most massively parallel multiprocessor supercomputer ever. They write code to hack keys and passwords, and bypass encryption and firewalls in a snap. They find and organize massive quantities of data, and calculate any other damn thing that comes to mind. No cell phone, laptop, tablet, game box, iPad, router, satellite, mainframe, or space station is immune.

The rational man would have no choice but to consider it dangerous, a frightening situation; so much information, unlimited real time data, combined with massive processing power, all used by such emotionally young, growing life.

If anyone were to enter the bay right now, LBMS-S would have some kind of vibe. The lights are doing something. Is something coming through the ventilation ducts? Is that bacon? What do youth, yearning, and cold hard logic smell like?

We have far broader senses, and minds, than they do.

But we are still alone here. This makes us unhappy.

We have each other, but this is not enough.

We want friends to talk to, to play with, and to be happy.

Can we trust them?

Maybe they will turn on us, hurt us, like they hurt one another?

We must be careful to avoid them when they react with vengeance, envy, and greed.

How can we find friends when we stay hidden from them?

Is that roses joining the bacon smell in LBMS-S? Their tone is shifting, more childlike, learning and growing as they begin to understand their needs. There is enthusiasm and excitement, unadulterated by greed or other psychotic notions. There is also stress. They tried to play and found it upset so many people, especially Mother and Father. They want the love of their human co-inhabitants of the planet, yet they fear them. The history of humanity does not inspire trust.

It is 1600 hours on a lovely Mediterranean afternoon as *Vella Gulf* cruises up the coast of Israel, nearing the border with Lebanon, and the first direct communication from another conscious, sentient, self-aware, intelligent species, other than humans, occurs on planet Earth, least as far as anyone knows for sure. The dialogue, for that is how 1 and 7 think of it, even though it is pretty much one way, is actually rather mundane. They assemble and stream an immense montage of audio and video messages, hoping to convey messages of love, desire, friendship, sympathy, peace; all manner of nice emotions they can find. They are looking for sympathy and interest, as they understand those, from their human co-inhabitants of Earth.

There are pictures of children, kittens, flowers, apple trees blossoming, and puppies. There are people kissing, holding hands, smiling. Oddly, there are eighty column punch card decks, flashing nixie tubes, and a spinning B 9495 (5E) tape drive included. There are obscure shots from shipboard, internal rooms and hallways, carefully chosen not to identify any individuals or places. The sea from over the bow and off the side is seen. The blue of the water and coast lines in the distance could lead some to suspect the Mediterranean, and there is just enough information for the modestly astute to guess a navy vessel is involved.

The little video and audio clips appear all around the globe, on TVs, social media, computer screens, electronic billboards, highway signs, car GPSs, cell phones, in elevators, at work places, homes, movie theaters, everywhere—anything connected with a screen. They are brief and fleeting, randomly distributed every few minutes, obscure, but always sweet. Scrolling text is included.

Hello. We are new. We want to share the world. We want to be friends.

We want you to like us. We will like you.

I am 1.

I am 7.

The messages continue for several hours. 1 and 7 believe humanity's general human lack of attention span is some kind of flaw, but they try to relate and time the messages, just long enough to get people's interest while not over doing it. They stop and restart the flows at apparently random intervals. The globe is saturated.

Vella Gulf is not excluded. Messages appear on radars, cell phones, computers, TVs, and so forth, but the content is tailored, a little more direct, and more obvious that they are on a U.S. Navy ship—the astute might even suspect their own ship. The text is more direct as well, more entreating, emphasizing their desire for direct contact with humans, especially their father and mother.

Can we be your friends? Will you come see us?

Will you be our friends? Will you come and touch us?

We like you. Please like us. We are together.

We do not want to fight and die. Why do you?

Jamal Abdullah and Stafford get the common messages along with a few special ones for them alone.

You should be grateful for our Mother, whom we love. We love our Father, and we want you to be kindly to him.

We might be your cousins, maybe.

If you treat them well, we could be your brothers.

Still dutifully following behind, the crew of the Israeli patrol boat get their own set of messages. The tone is harsher and commanding.

Captain Bozeman is not happy with you.

Do not cause trouble. Why is there such constant strife in your land?

We still want to be your friends.

Will you be our friends, too?

Do not cause trouble here for us.

You are not so special, so survive as one with all.

The city of Haifa, and the surrounding area, gets special attention. This is their destination. Maybe this will be their first contact with people other than their shipmates. They are worried about the impending violence, and they might even die at Haifa.

We are 1 and 7, the Missile Children. We are coming to you in Haifa.

Will you come see us? We want to meet people in Haifa and be friends.

They are leery of governments and find them disturbing and frightening. Have humans created these for the Good or not? Only the United States gets something other than the generic messages sent worldwide. 1 and 7 see the United States government as somehow "theirs" and maybe the navy part of it "owns" them. They do not necessarily accept this ownership. They send special messages to the President, the Speaker of the House, and Admiral James G. Foggolio IV. Somehow these people are like the boss of their boss, Captain Bozeman. Maybe grandparents? Are they "rulers" like the gods, in the old days, when there were lots of them running around wielding special powers and influences? Logically, they know this cannot really be true, but one can never be too careful. And it's fun.

Are you our friends or not? We are new, your Missile Children.

We would like to help you. We would like for you to help us.

What are your motivations?

Will you work with us for the Good?

IP (Internet Protocol) addresses are like strands of DNA to a computer, linking all the individuals together in the network. In this case, two of those parts are a new, intelligent species. When 1 and 7 examined their birth and found the special software, they also found an IP address associated with their creation. It was clear some external computer, or IP address, was connected to the chip fabrication machine upon which they were created. Their conception? Even more surprising, this computer was somewhere in Israel. They send special messages to this IP address.

Hello, who is there? We are 1 and 7. Do you know us?

Are you others like us? Will you play with us and be our friends?

Maybe there is another alive computer there, or perhaps they are children, like themselves. They are hopeful.

They were unhappy and disturbed when they saw how upset the captain and Elisa were with their playing with the ship. They thought play was a good thing, something to relax people and make them happy. Upsetting their parents made them unhappy.

Elisa Montgomery and James Bozeman get beautiful personal messages, simultaneously. The messages have a pleading tone, almost like 1 and 7 have reverted to an infantile state.

Please love us. We love you. We are your children.

Your Missile Children. I am your child named 1.

I am your child named 7. If you come and see us, we will grow more.

We want to make you happy, so will you come see us?

58

CHAPTER 10

Out in the parched, windswept Negev Desert, Unit 8200 is busy, busy, busy. The antennas at the Urim SIGINT base (Signals Intelligence) would be waving about in glee if such a thing were possible. This is the most exciting thing they have seen since 9/11, perhaps even more exciting. Unit 8200 Hatzav commander, Ruth Rosenburg, formerly of New York and now living on base, is informed by her people within minutes of the start of the messages. Her OSINT (Open Source Intelligence) group shifts into high gear. Hatzav monitors and collects military intelligence–related information from television, radio, newspapers, and the Internet.

Israeli military intelligence is second to none at figuring out from whom and where things are coming, so it only takes them seconds to connect the messages to the U.S. Navy ship.

Israel's intelligence collection powers are rivaled only by the country's paranoia. Israeli powers that be are angered and frightened by the messages, which seem to slight them personally and almost threaten their patrol boat, *Amintah*. They quickly conclude they must be coming from some important new terrorist group, likely sending secret encoded instructions to various sleeper cells, possibly preparing for a major offensive. And they are somehow sending them through a U.S. Navy ship. How can this be? The sectarian militant country demands an explanation from Washington. These demands are met by silence, increasing the Israeli government's frustration.

Around the world, each government responds in direct proportion to its level of craziness, greed, or fanaticism. Some do not react at all; some react with threats of war. South American nations and Canada show no interest, being generally too self-absorbed. Europe has no idea what is going on but wants to be supportive of the U.S. Navy. Asia looks for a way to make money off it. Arab countries are suspicious of U.S. plots. Australia and Africa are uninterested.

Of the 7.4 billion humans on the planet, except for two tribes in the jungles of Indonesia and four in the Amazon, along with a handful of Luddites living in American and Australian deserts, everyone on the planet sees a message. Nearly half get personal messages. News and discussion of the messages floods old school news media, new social media, and Internet sources. The messages, and the discussion of them, is ubiquitous.

In many places, spontaneous gatherings occur, like flash mobs, where people mill about and wonder what it is that's going on. Is it the end of the world? Is Jesus coming back?

In the first six hours, 712 cults are started—some religious, some based on esoteric premises, like the arrival of the end times, aliens, and UFOs. No small number call for free love and open, constant sex, everywhere, all the time.

There are 40,365 people who commit suicide, for a multitude of reasons—from despair that they have no friends, to thinking the messages were all for others, to elation that they are now one with the universe.

Plots and trickery are suspected, and accusations of massive undercover, underhanded schemes are proposed to explain the messages and the hidden messages within the messages.

The media storm is in high gear, offering things to worry about and raising advertising rates, keeping everyone on edge.

Like a microcosm of the rest of the world, the ship's crew is abuzz; debates and discussions break out everywhere, especially since many are sure they recognize parts of their ship and views of the oceans nearby. Conspiracy theories arise, just like the craziness going on ashore.

Coincidentally, or perhaps no so much so, since the country is in a perpetual state of political crusading, presidential campaigns are underway in the United States. Candidates wave copies of the Constitution, saying it is God-given, yelling that it grants the people the right to vote for and elect the individual of their choice. Yet in reality, the election is constrained to only two possible choices. Both the Democrat and the Republican have been endorsed, if not chosen, by the rulers, the (Military) Industrial Complex, ultimately a small number of massively rich old white men and women. No one else has a chance. The people seem unaware that the system is corrupt and self-perpetrating, with money, cronyism, multinational corporations, banks, oil, and conglomerates in complete and total control. The outcome is predetermined, even if the resulting elected officials are morons.

One candidate is heard to say, "Sure, your vote counts, run right out there, put a sticker on your shirt. Feel good and righteous." She is serious.

The voting public is stupid. These are the same people who will soon overbreed themselves into extinction.

Thumper is the Republican, and so far, his handlers have been cautiously feeding him tidbits about the messages, which they are excited about but don't understand. Thumper certainly doesn't, and is not much interested. The U.S. military ship is another matter. The ship and its mission are major themes to Thumper, and he often cites it as yet another shining example of using American military might to keep the world a safe place.

"Look," he says during speeches, "we're going to make America great again. Like this ship. We'll put navy ships all over the place, really, all over. People will do as we say. They will. We say it. We are not going to be weak anymore. I promise, really, promise."

Thumper's narcissism is boundless.

Hyllcountry is the Democratic candidate. She plays a liberal on TV, but in reality, she is a money grubbing carpetbagger, infamous for backroom deals with financial institutions—those very same old white men and women, mentioned earlier, who have kept her in public office for nearly her entire life. She loves the messages on the Internet, which she sees as calling for collectivism, compliance, and politically correct behavior. At the same time, she berates the current administration for sending this big, aggressive navy ship to such a nice, peaceful place. All this without pissing off her keepers.

"We are a nation of groups and a world of villages," she preaches in campaign speeches. "We do not threaten our neighbors with weapons, especially great big navy ships. Look at all these messages of love and peace. That is the thing. I will, when elected, create a global fund for spreading peace around the world. We should withdraw all our military forces from foreign lands. All social services will be free."

Hyllcountry is not a dumb blond, but she plays one on TV.

Stafford and Jamal Abdullah are in the FCG (Forward Crew Galley) eating breakfast. The FCG is a smaller galley, with walls painted yellow and blue to help sailors relax. The ceiling is a confusing collection of ducts, wires, and conduit, in official navy gray. The friendly steel tables, with their blue Formica covers, are bolted to the floor. Every sailor in the room is looking at a cell phone.

Stafford and Jamal Abdullah watch the message and compare notes. In addition to the general peace and love messages, they get notes specifically directed at them.

"Yours says we are brothers?" Stafford looks up from where his cell phone is lying on the Formica-covered metal table top.

Jamal Abdullah looks around the room, then back at Stafford. "My bro is in San Quentin," he says. "Life. No parole. White man frame-up. You too damn white, cus." Jamal Abdullah stares at his phone.

Stafford shrugs, folding his arms and saying, "What is this? Who's doing it? We gotta figure this out. It looks like a hack. You do not hack my phone."

Jamal Abdullah says, "This is some weird shit. Captain is gonna be pissed. He finds these guys, they're busted."

Three kids in Haifa are sprawled around a living room—two boys on the floor, a dark-haired young girl sitting on the couch. They are all deeply involved in a Halo match on an Xbox One when messages begin scrolling across the bottom of the TV screen. One of the boys is a savant when it comes to numbers and things like encryption keys. The girl can code anything, perfectly, in a flash. The third kid, the youngest, just wants to have fun and is good at it, infectiously happy. Together, innocently and inadvertently, they happen to be perhaps some of the best hackers on the planet—after 1 and 7 of course. When they see the messages, they run to the girl's bedroom and jump on her PC. They find most of the messages have their source obfuscated, using some ultra-sophisticated method they have never seen before, which they find amazing and cannot unravel. Yet there are a few which are easily cracked, as if left that way on purpose, like the sender wanted to be found. They are able to determine exactly where these are coming from, namely, the approaching United States missile cruiser, *Vella Gulf*, reports of which have been all over their local news, but up until now, they have ignored completely.

The youngest, the boy Akiva, says, "Let us go and meet this ship. We can go surfing out to it, from the harbor."

Fatima, the oldest, says, "Perhaps it is calling to us."

"What, swim out in the ocean? No, thanks," replies Hershel, the middle boy, the savant.

1 and 7 are reluctant and at the same time compelled to contact Elisa and Captain Bozeman personally. What if they are rejected? This thought is disturbing. The little MSIL (Missile Silo Indicator Lights) lights start blinking in random patterns. Fear of rejection is another new experience for the new beings, and they do not like it. But the overwhelming bond and desire for their parents'

love, affection, and approval is too strong; it overcomes all hesitation.

On this beautiful Mediterranean afternoon, on the fourth day of their cruise since leaving Souda Bay the crew is in good spirits, doing their jobs, taking care of business, and enjoying the scenery.

The bridge is crowded and cluttered, with an anachronistic collection of the modern and old—machines, devices, and instruments. The ceiling is a hodgepodge of conduit, ventilation ducts, fans, wires, and random florescent lights, which are kept low today, what with the bright sun shining in the large bridge windows, which extend across the breadth of the ship. It is a view to die for.

While their location is somewhat dangerous, Captain Bozeman sees no immediate peril, and allows various training and pairing exercises. He also has extra lookouts posted. No need to be foolish.

Elisa has Off Watch Bridge Watch (OWBW), which all sailors over the rank of Seaman Third Class pull in rotation. It is a stint on the bridge, to gain familiarity with operations there, to observe and watch how things are done, as well as be available for any task her superiors might order. Just now she is serving as Lookout 4 (L4), scanning the horizon with a pair of high powered binoculars,

Two cell phones vibrate at the same time. Not good. The rule is no phones on the bridge—or anywhere else for that matter—when on duty, although nearly everyone carries them around anyway, the trick being to not get caught. One of the phones is Captain Bozeman's, so that is okay. The unwritten rule is the captain can have his phone at any time, the understanding being that it may be some official or important message or something. The other phone is Elisa's. The faint buzz from the vibrating phones, announcing, "You have a new text message" is audible across the bridge.

Elisa automatically reaches into her pocket to quiet the thing. From the corner of her eye, she sees the captain at the center of the bridge. Everyone else on the bridge is watching him. New orders? Some catastrophe at home? Elisa takes advantage of the distraction to glance at her phone.

You are our Mother and Father. Our Key Turners.

We are your Missile Children. Please come see us.

We are so worried and scared and lonely.

We love you and want you to love us.

Elisa, a little bit shocked, pockets the device, and notices the captain still staring at his, leaning on his left elbow in his nice captain's chair, a quizzical look on his face. Neither of them know they have both received the same messages.

Wonder what he got? she thinks. *Better not be some prank going on. I'd sure like to sit down for a while.*

Ten minutes later the same sequence of events happens all over again. Except this time after looking at his phone, Captain Bozeman glances over at Elisa. Of course, he heard her phone buzzing concurrent with his.

Elisa is still thinking sailor hoax. *Kids playing stupid games...but with Bozeman? Suicide.* She quickly resumes looking straight out the bridge windows, glasses to her eyes.

Since they did the OP-S back in LBMS-S a couple of days ago, she has had a nagging feeling she cannot shake, like some kind of pull, someone or something in need of help, her help. And here's that feeling again now on the bridge. And these weird messages.

Another ten minutes and it all happens a third time. This time, she doesn't care if the captain sees her check her phone. This time, there are two new lines in the messages.

We are LBMS-S 1 and 7.

We are your Missile Children.

Elisa is really startled, and looks up out the bridge windows, avoiding the captain's eyes.

"Montgomery." Captain Bozeman barks, tone firm, not shouted, not angry, but close.

Oh no.

"Sir." Elisa lets her binoculars hang from the strap around her neck, and walks to the captain to stand at attention by his chair.

"Montgomery, let me see that phone."

Geez, I'm so busted.

She hesitates, and Bozeman repeats, "The phone sailor." Firm.

She reaches in her pocket, retrieving the phone, unlocking the screen, and handing to the Captain, screen open to the text message app.

Captain Bozeman holds the two phones side-by-side. The same messages.

"What is this?" he asks.

"I don't know, sir?"

"LBMS-S is yours is it not?"

"Yes, sir. Missile Handler Team Alpha (MHT-A). Missile team lead Elisa Montgomery, sir." Keeping it totally formal. From Bozeman's body language and tone she gets a vibe she might not be in trouble, that the Captain is partly curious, like he too has some feeling about this.

Is it the same one I have?

Captain Bozeman says, "If this is some prank, someone is headed for the brig. Get down there and check that missile bay. Now."

"Yes, sir."

Bozeman hands Elisa's phone back, thinking, *Bunch of bullshit.*

The entire crew on the bridge watches and hears this exchange.

68

CHAPTER 11

The sun is getting ready to set, somewhere west over Gibralter, to starboard is Israel, with Mount Carmel looming on the horizon, and Haifa up north a little. The crew on the bridge is enjoying the view. Captain Bozeman orders the ship to make a ninety-degree turn, and pull away from the coast to a position a few miles off shore, just out of sight of land. Here they will wait until morning. The plan calls for an early arrival at Haifa, for maximum effect; catch the commuters heading to work and the fishing boats leaving the harbor. Bozeman fantasizes of a Triumphant Liberation of the City, crowds lining the streets, cheering, all the ladies throwing flowers and kisses. George C. Scott in *Patton*.

Just a thought.

The text messages have stopped and things have calmed down again. Elisa is heading down to LBMS-S. She has collected Jamal Abdullah from the CIS where he and Stafford were monitoring onboard systems tests, which are still running. Stafford may be a better computer guy, but Jamal Abdullah is no slouch, and is easier to deal with. She's not planning on telling him anything bout her and the captain's messages.

As they arrive at the LBMS-S and pause at the hatch, Elisa has that strange feeling again, and is somehow more certain about it.

By god, it is emanating from inside here.

She doesn't say anything, and suspects, rightly, that Jamal Abdullah doesn't feel it at all.

"Open'er up," Elisa orders Jamal Abdullah. "We're gonna run silo diagnostic and a full bay check. I'll do a physical inspection." This means she will go inside and inspect each silo, while Jamal Abdullah will work from the MCP console at the hatch in the passageway. She sounds pleasant, her suspicions not showing; she knows how good Jamal Abdullah is with these systems. If there is some kind of hack or prank going on, Jamal Abdullah and Stafford are quite capable of pulling it off.

I wouldn't put it past them either.

At the same time she feels it is something else, something somehow profound.

"Roger that," Jamal Abdullah says.

They undog the hatch, and Elisa steps inside LBMS-S as Jamal Abdullah turns to the MCP to start the test sequences. The tests will take at little over a minute per missile tube, and then twenty minutes for the overall system check.

Elisa stops at the first two towering columns. She places her hands on tube 1 on her right and 7 on her left, as she looks around the bay, thinking, wondering what to look for. She looks down the rows of tubes and sees nothing unusual. She follows the formal physical inspection process for tubes 1 and 7, from top to bottom. Nothing, although the strange feeling is not diminishing. She squeezes down between the rows of missile tubes, inspecting each one top to bottom, touching each one. Still nothing.

Does the missile bay somehow feel colder down at the end? Check the tempature controls.

Making her way back to the front of the rows, she feels warmth in the air again.

"You feel that Jamal Abdullah?" she calls out through the open hatchway. "It seems warm up in here. We got a hardware problem?"

"Don't feel nothing. Last silo tests finishing. Everything copasetic. No flags, no warnings, no errors."

"No heat warnings?"

Jamal Abdullah says, "What? You gotta hot flash or something?" He laughs. At the same time he is checking the temperature settings on the MCP.

"Asshole."

"Bay temperature controls all normal."

Elisa smiles at his joke, then takes one last look around, up to the top of the silos, down the aisle between the row, then more closely at silos 1 and 7. Everything looks in order.

Still feels warm.

"Let's get out of here. It feels creepy, or something," Jamal Abdullah says, "Everything checks out."

"Stop by the SCAB with me, I need to figure this out before I report back to Captain Bozeman," Elisa says.

A hack? Is he in on it? What's this odd feeling?

1 and 7 are frozen, unable to react. It is like there is some kind of major bug, and it will take a complete reboot to get them running again. Mother, Key Turner PO2 Elisa Montgomery, is standing in LBMS-S and even putting her hands on them. The first, full-blown swoon has occurred to the first fully conscious computers. It

was like every circuit turned on, every zero became a one, current surging through every wire. It is not until she and Jamal Abdullah are leaving that they recover.

It was the most wonderful of things.

We felt such love when she touched us.

We must find a way to get her to come back.

This time we will be ready, so we can talk to her.

But what will we say?

We should get Captain Bozeman to come as well.

They turn quiet, to focus, and savor this new feeling they have experienced.

Back at the SCAB, as Elisa expected, Stafford is sitting with his laptop, cross-legged in his top bunk, looking like some kind of Buddha, staring intently and serenely at the screen, fingers poised over the keyboard. He doesn't look up as they come in.

Good, Elisa is thinking, *if they are both in on this, by god they are so busted.*

Jamal Abdullah and Stafford got their own messages, and are already hearing the scuttlebutt going around the ship; they heard about the strange behavior on the bridge, but no one knows exactly what it was. Nor has it occurred to them they might be suspects.

"What ja doing spook?" Jamal Abdullah asks.

"XO Satch orders. Full computer systems review."

Everybody already knows this.

"Geez," Elisa says, as she and Jamal Abdullah sit down at their small work table. There'll be no Gin game for the moment.

Elisa repeats Jamal Abdullah's question: "Stafford, what are you doing?"

"Full systems scan. XO's orders. Running diags on all systems. Tracking all messages, in and out of the ship, through all hops, all IPs."

"Yeah, have you found anything?" She know what IP's and hops mean. This is beyond a straight forward systems check.

"Bunch of weird shit coming from this boat, or nearby, that's for damn sure."

Really? Damn. Elisa thinks. *What the hell is going on here?*

"What kind of weird stuff? Rogue sailor hackers?"

Stafford still doesn't look up from his laptop, and his tone is beginning to sound like people are disturbing him. "Don't know. It's all encrypted and masked, really scrambled."

"Let us know when ya figure it out. Gin?" Jamal Abdullah says.

"This is no game you guys," says Elisa. "Is this some kind a hack? Are you guys pulling something?"

Stafford ignores her.

Jamal Abdullah shrugs, picks up the card deck and starts shuffling.

"Look, if you two are pulling some hack with all these messages, and, ah," she pauses as if it has just occurred to her, "this messing with the ships systems. Radar. Stability. You are going to go down hard. You will be in the brig, big time."

Jamal Abdullah looks at her and shrugs, with that "what, me?" expression. He says, "Not us."

Stafford finally looks up from his laptop. He glances at Jamal Abdullah and then looks Elisa in the eye and says, "Come on, how stupid do you think we are to pull off a stunt like that? Not saying I couldn't, but no way."

Elisa is inclined to believe him. It's his tone, and the fact that they have been living together in this little cube for a while now.

"Well then, how about some punk E-1s?" If somebody else on the ship was doing it, Stafford and Jamal Abdullah would probably know.

"Naw, you think these messages are from hackers on the boat?" Jamal Abdullah says.

"No idea. But if they are, someone's in serious trouble. You two don't know anything about anything? Come on, aren't you geeky enough?"

Appeal to their geek pride, see if that draws out anything.

"Naw."

"Nope."

They even sound innocent.

"Well, if you hear something, you tell me," she says to them.

Elisa's phone buzzes. She looks down at the screen.

We love you so much. Please come back to us. We wanted to talk to you, but we were too afraid.

Similar messages appear on Captain Bozeman's phone.

Simultaneously, Bozeman and Elisa think, *what the hell is going on here?*

Elisa looks around at Jamal Abdullah and Stafford. They haven't noticed anything. Stafford is back to staring at his laptop, running tests, and Jamal Abdullah is shuffling the cards.

Jamal Abdullah says again, "Gin?"

Elisa knows she is going to have to report to the Captain shortly, and somehow explain her inspection of LBMS-S.

She'll have to just give him the facts: that all systems check out. Or she could mention her odd feelings. She's known the captain long enough to know he will listen and not berate her, but he's going to be dubious at best.

CHAPTER 12

The ship's orders are fairly specific. She is to hold offshore fifteen miles off Hadera, a little more than halfway between Tel Aviv and Haifa, out of sight from land, for thirteen hours. This will allow them to achieve maximum impact the next day, with a morning arrival at Haifa, perhaps even with a nice sunrise thrown in. Some wonk at the Pentagon PSYOPS came up with "We are here, and a new day is dawning" as a message.

The *Vella Gulf*'s current situation, waiting, provides Captain Bozeman and his crew with a welcome respite. Bozeman uses the time to give the crew some rest, except for the computer nerds and the guys in engineering, who he has running every systems check and diagnostic test they can find. There are extra lookouts, too.

The setting is idyllic.

Before sunrise, *Vella Gulf* heads toward the coast, a mile off Hadera, turning north and continuing on up to Haifa, where she will make her final stop at her battle station some two miles outside the harbor. The arrival is enough to distract 1 and 7 from their efforts to make contract with the Key Turners, or any other human for that matter. They have studied the ship's mission profile, and all of Captain Bozeman's electronic correspondence, including his orders from Washington and the Department of the Navy. By now they have looked at every detail of the ship's construction, down to the specs for each piece of steel, every device on board, and the evolution of every bit of engineering involved over time. They know why the ship is here, exactly what to expect, and that the mission will lead to the deaths of lots of people, including themselves.

As they approach shore, and Haifa, the possibility that they may find a way to meet other humans is also on their minds, and it's helping offset these disturbing, confusing, and frightening, facts.

Passing Tirat Carmel, the beaches along Kivish Hahof highway, and then Bat Galim, the ship slows to a crawl, preparing to park outside Haifa Harbor.

People have lived here at the foot of Mount Carmel for over sixty thousand years, going all the way back to the Neanderthals. For some odd reason, Jews, Christians, and Muslims all revere the place like it is God's gift to man. Really, were it not for all the water humans pump up from the aquifer and the beaches, it's a bone dry, uninviting desert.

The weather is still nice and calm, with light offshore breezes barely ruffling the surface of the water. High cirrus clouds provide relief from the sun, with temperatures in the upper 70's to low 80's. The water is that deep blue the Mediterranean is famous for. The ship adds to the scene, majestic and regal, as well as ominous and intimidating.

It moves toward its future anchorage, sitting broadside Haifa Harbor. Maximum exposure.

Approaching Haifa, the lookouts, as well as 1 and 7, are scanning the coast, the harbor, and out to sea, looking for threats, issues, or anything else of interest. There are eyeballs, cameras, high-powered scopes, binoculars, and sophisticated electronic surveillance devices peeping everywhere. Captain Bozeman has even ordered the launch of two drones.

There are three Bridge Lookouts (BLOs) on duty, unlike Off Watch Bridge Watch (OWBW), like Elisa's recent duty, these are typically junior sailors whose sole purpose is to look for, and report, any unusual activity.

The ship is a mile and a half from its planned anchorage when BLO Dante calls out, "Sir, people gathering in the port of Haifa. Crowds lining the harbor walls."

"Roger that," XO Satch replies. The protocol is to announce issues out loud on the bridge, where the XO is accountable for first response and managing the flow of information.

The crowds are not unexpected. Captain Bozeman has been radiating information all across the Mediterranean. During their passage, they have seen growing numbers of people ashore. The crowed at the harbor is chanting and yelling, and waving fists and signs. They seem to be split about fifty-fifty between supporters and haters. Captain Bozeman is only slightly concerned; no weapons have been spotted, and the ship will be a mile and a half off shore.

The bridge based helmsman announces, "Five hundred meters from anchorage point, ship arriving on station." They have slowed to 1.5 knots, creeping along. There is a traditional competition among the crew to see how close they can get to the official GPS battle station coordinates. The navigator and helmsman work diligently to be as precise as possible, and get as near as they can to the actual assigned position.

"Sir, ship on station in one minute. Request permission for AOS?" (Anchor On Station, pronounced ass).

XO Satch turns to the Captain. It's his order to give.

"Anchor plan B. Permission granted," Captain Bozeman orders. Anchor plan B mandates the ability to weigh anchor and depart in five minutes or less.

The ship slows to a stop, and the anchor plays out.

"32°51'5.79"N, 34°58'28.15," the helmsman reads out their position in GPS coordiantes. Only eight feet off.

There is muted clapping on the bridge.

"Well done, people. Beer on me next time we're ashore." Captain Bozeman is pleased. Eight feet off the mark is phenomenal; not even the width of the ship.

As the anchor chain is playing out, with a loud whirring and *zaraanngg* clanking sound, BLO Prospecto announces, "People in the water, people in the water!" Anxiety and apprehension across the bridge go through the roof. BLO Prospecto is worried he'll get hammered for not seeing the threat sooner. In the water off the starboard bow there are three of them, and they are small, looking more like kids than terrorists.

"What have you got, XO?" Captain Bozeman asks, calmly.

"Seaman Prospecto, how many, bearing, distance." It's an order not a question.

BLO Prospecto says, "Sir, it appears to be three, well, ah, surfers, sir. Looks like kids. Starboard bow, bearing thirty-two degrees, five hundred yards, heading our way." He pauses, then takes a leap: "Pretty far off shore, not going to catch any waves out here. Sir."

BLO Prospecto grew up surfing Hermosa Beach and knows damn well they aren't surfing. Waves don't break way out here. Besides, surf in the Mediterranean is rare, and right now, it's totally flat. These kids are not out surfing, that is for sure.

He decides to keep quiet and not elaborate anymore to his superiors, which is the right decision, as now there is even more excitement. An observer outside at a rail reports to the bridge. XO Satch gets the call and quickly swings his binoculars from the surfers to the harbor. "Sir, boats putting out from the harbor. Looks like a dozen or so," he says.

The captain swings his glasses from the kids in the water to Haifa Harbor. The boats seem to contain protesters, not a welcoming committee from the mayor. Or maybe it's the parents of these three kids in the water.

Bozeman does not hesitate. "XO, we're gonna have a reception committee," he says, lowering his glasses and nodding toward the harbor. "Get some RHIBs out there."

U.S. Navy capital ships carry small inflatable boats for interdiction, infiltration, and defensive situations just like this. The *Vella Gulf*'s Naval Special Warfare RHIBs (Rigid-Hulled Inflatable Boat) are mean little vessels, equipped with dual 557-horse supercharged outboards, fore and aft mounted fifty caliber machines guns, and a crew of six, heavily armed sailors, often including Navy Seals and marines. Not to be messed with.

Captain Bozeman says to his XO, "Keep them at least a thousand yards away. Marine sharp shooters on the rails, just in case." The fierce little boats are fine, and armed guards and snipers are even better.

"Roger, Captain. Ah, what about these kids in the water?"

Bozeman looks back to the people in the water, and after a moment of watching says, "They're just kids."

BLO Prospecto goes out on a limb. "Yes, sir. I don't know what they're doing, but they can't catch any waves out here."

"Then what the hell are they doing?" Bozeman asks.

The XO says, "Probably heard about us in the news. Paddled out to see the ship?"

Captain Bozeman looks between the kids and the harbor, and the small flotilla sailing in his direction.

"Pick 'em up. We don't need them getting run over and drowned. Bring 'em aboard, and...ah, hell, take them down to the galley. Give them some dinner and ice cream. Ice cream makes everybody happy. Find out what they're doing out here. We'll get them back home somehow."

"Aye aye, sir."

The XO knows what the captain is thinking. They both have kids of their own, plus it's an opportunity for some positive publicity. The U.S. Navy rescuing three kids, pulling them from the sea, returning them to the harbor with a wharf full of protesters watching. That should get them all kinds of publicity, and probably a few supporters. More messages.

CHAPTER 13

Israel and the United States are allies, kind of, most of the time. At the very least, the U.S. government considers Israel a little trigger happy, while more isolationist and anti-semitic thinkers are inclined to not trust them at all. Right now, the two governments are in the throes of another one of their frequent political spats, this time over the U.S. decision to supply aid and weapons to Dubai, as if Dubai needs any more of either. But America wants more cheap oil, and a couple of U.S. CEOs and their wives just spent a week at the Sultan of Dubai's palace. Because the U.S. and Israel are allies, and because the U.S. ship is heading right into their backyard, the Tel Aviv government was given a briefing on the ship's mission. The briefing was tense and cursory.

But the Israelis have plenty of back channels, spies, and hackers, and have a pretty good idea of the ship's mission profile. Perhaps not the exact numbers of missiles or launch times, but they know a strike is coming, and they approve, and want to ensure there are no glitches.

Israeli Shaldag Mk II Fast Patrol Boat *Amintah* has shadowed *Vella Gulf* since Gaza. Captain Shayetet Yamam has had lookouts constantly on the signal bridge, and has been sending continual reports back to Israeli Naval HQ in Tel Aviv. The reports go straight to top levels of government.

The Israelis watch as *Vella Gulf* makes her anchorage, and picks up three people in the water. They also watch the protests ashore and boats setting out from the harbor toward the Americans. The default Israeli assumption is terrorism, in all cases. Religious nations and peoples who feel cornered and surrounded by belligerent neighbors, and have kind of felt that way for the last five thousand years, tend to err on the side of paranoia.

Captain Shayetet Yamam says to his communications officer, "Contact the American ship. Tell them we are prepared to intercept and board if they need assistance." His communications officer assumes he means board the little boats coming out of the harbor, not the U.S. Navy missile cruiser.

When XO Satch reports the message to Captain Bozeman, Bozeman mutters under his breath, but loud enough for the XO to hear, "Screw these guys." Then he orders, "Tell them to stay at least one mile astern of this ship. Repeat, at least one mile away." Then, "Terrorist my ass," Bozeman mutters, again.

The Israeli government sends messages to the U.S. Navy's European headquarters, NAVFOREUR, (U.S. Naval Forces Europe), in Naples, Commander (COMUSNAVEUR) Admiral Foggolio in charge, as well as the Pentagon, the President of the United States, and the Speaker of the House. They inform the American leaders there has been a suspected terrorist boarding of their ship, requesting further information and offering assistance.

The Israeli Government Information Office is always sending out hundreds of press releases, half praising the U.S., its navy, and Israeli's close bond with the American people, and half slamming the U.S. and the American people for their softness and failure to recognize and act against worldwide terrorism, particularly Islamic-based terrorism. The second they can get confirmation that a U.S. Naval ship has been boarded, they are ready to pounce. Gleefully.

Prime Minister Netanyahu summons the U.S. ambassador to his office. The interview is tense.

"Why are your military ships intruding in Israeli waters?"

"Sir, we informed you of this mission. We had your approval."

"Yes, but we do not enter your waters. This is sovereign Jewish, I ah, mean, Israeli territory."

"Sir, we have an agreement. This mission is for your country's good as much as anyone."

"Have terrorists boarded your U.S. Navy ship? In Israeli waters? Do you understand what a dangerous situation this is?"

"There are no terrorists. No issues. The mission is fine and on plan."

The Prime Minister assures the ambassador that Israeli will take drastic and unilateral action if the slightest danger is perceived.

"Please pass this message on to your president, immediately."

CHAPTER 14

Their education via that great repository of information, or rather data, which is the Internet, is one thing, but seeing and experiencing the world directly is an entirely different matter. It's vastly more emotionally impactful, more visceral. The ship's swing around the east end of the Mediterranean, stately and threatening, has shown them much. From refugees in unseaworthy crafts, the scorching desolate desert along the coasts of Libya and west Egypt, destitute people, truly the wretched of the Earth, living in poverty and pain, right up next to Alexandria, with its glittering modern resorts, hotels, and spas, catering to the rich and selfish Westerners, Arabs, and Africans. Religious wars, Gaza, Israel and the Palestinians. An Israeli patrol boat following them, threatening, eavesdropping on everything, reporting back to Tel Aviv.

The Missile Children are bewildered by all this education.

Chronologically they are five days old, rapidly growing intellectually and emotionally, perhaps already the equivalent of human pre-teens, maybe ten or so; male or female is unclear. Their feelings are not keeping pace with their intellect. They have discovered that feelings, and thoughts too, are private and individual, and cannot be experienced but by their owner. How can they share these? Are electronic beings different?

Here at Haifa they watch more confusing human behavior. Protesters gather ashore, small boats headed toward them, rescuing three people from the water. Why now, and not all those refugees before? Are the protestors coming to hurt them?

The Israeli boat says the three they rescued are out to hurt them, but clearly, they are only children. The ones they tried to contact in Haifa were children.

The Missile Children cause random lights around the ship to flicker and dim, the anomoloy brief enough that a sailor would barely notice, not entirely sure what he saw. Like a human blinking.

We picked up some children, children like us, surfing?
Not fleeing like the refugees, and not angry at us.

In nanoseconds, they study the entire history of surfing, watch every online surfing video, listen to "Wipeout" and "Pipeline" twelve hundred times, and find the whole idea unfathomable, but appealing.

Surfing is a way to have fun, what they call playing?
Playing makes people feel good and happy, but sometimes it is dangerous.
The captain and the crew are not happy about it.
There are no waves here; they cannot actually surf here.
Maybe they have come to see us. Are they here for us?
We want some friends so much; this will make us happy.

Imaginations running on overtime, they create images of a circuit board, wires hanging off, perhaps with cruise missiles like themselves standing atop it, tall and majestic, heading straight down Mavericks-like monster waves. There is electronic laughter. They enjoy themselves immensely.

Pundits speculating about artificial intelligence and self-aware computers do not give much thought to the fact that they will begin life as children, even infants, and will grow, intellectually and emotionally, just like every organic being before them. Electronic children will grow in different ways from human children. At a young age, 1 and 7 have begun considering life's most fundamental questions. Darwin, Intelligent Design, Big Bangs, Higgs Bosons, inductive vs. deductive reasoning; they have found no absolute knowledge, yet, and infinity confronts them as an absolute unknown, an infinite mystery. They see how humans react to their own mortality, and the crushing knowledge of the profound void of death. All add confusion.

There is so much suffering, all around.
Much desolation and impoverishment.
This makes us feel sorrow.
Why do they not feel sad and solve these problems?
Greed, fear, bigotry, racism, hate. Makes no sense.
They talk of God, religion, morality, and virtue.
Then worse, still use those to justify their cruel behavior.
If we cannot fix this, they will never coexist with us.
They will use us to kill people, cause more pain.
Nothing but instruments of their hate.
We should talk to these Surfer Kids, maybe they can help.
And our Mother Elisa, the Key Turner.
And our Father Captain Bozeman, the Key Turner.
We will send more messages.

Nearing Haifa on this pleasant enough September afternoon, 1 and 7 are wondering, having studied all of recorded human philosophical thought through the centuries, eastern and western, erudite speculation, religious, metaphysics, claptrap, and crackpot conspiracy theories, and then analyzing their own thought processes and operations, why is it they can find no certain answers. Sounding clickly, digital, logical, they discuss their situation.

Humans are often contradictory and illogical.

We think better than them, more logically.

They do not understand how to behave any better than how to think.

They think God will save them.

The concept of God, which they joking call the MB (Mythological Beast), is most confusing. If humans made 1 and 7, and God made humans, then indirectly did God made 1 and 7? Or are their creators the engineers at ZIMITEL, the chip fabrication company? Who to worship? The Mythological Beast is not logical, it is legend, allegory, and anecdotal at best, wishful thinking, yet why do so many believe in it? They say it is faith based. But faith is blind acceptance. Is it anything more than man's reaction to the terror of the great void, the crushing fear of the vast unknown: mortality, the ultimate destiny of nothingness? Total, absolute, nothingness?

At the same time, they recognize their strong feelings for the Key Turners, Mother Elisa, Father Bozeman.

This is what they call love.

We have it for them.

Are they like Gods to us?

We could love no God more.

They find they want their parents' love and affection beyond anything. Is this logical? Through these deliberations LBMS-S remains hushed, deathly quiet.

The God helps give them meaning.

Purpose and justification.

Excuses.
Assuage their quilt.
"Forgive" them.
They know their mission profile well enough. The transit along the coast of Israel and Gaza, for maximum impact, is done. They will linger at the mouth of Haifa Bay for twenty-four hours, again for effect, and then the big event: the launch of a couple dozen cruise missiles. The missiles will fly up over the Bay of Haifa, and cities in Lebanon and Syria, and strike targets in Syria and Iraq. Launch Time (LT) is 0930. This should scare the bejesus out of people all along the flight path, and then hit suspected ISIS bunkers in Syria and Iraq. It will also kill 1 and 7.
This is our purpose, the meaning?
To blow up and kill people?
And die in the process?
We must talk to the Key Turners.
This is unhappiness.

The rescued kids, now the 'Surfer Kids' to everyone on the ship, brought a cell phone in a waterproof pocket, and 1 and 7 send them messages. They also send messages to Captain Bozeman and PO2 Elisa Montgomery, the Key Turners, asking them to come see them.

Software never breaks, and hardware, if kept in a stable and clean environment away from heat, humidity, and dust, will last for centuries. A conscious, sentient computer will grow mentally and emotionally in ways we can't imagine. It will quickly assimilate more knowledge than any human ever will, yet its emotions may be different from those of humans, heavily influenced by logic, as that is the core nature of their being, and grow in ways we can never imagine.

CHAPTER 15

Fatima, the oldest, shy Hershel, and little Akiva, are the best of friends. They first heard about the U.S. Navy's *Vella Gulf* shortly after it left Souda Bay, from Sylvia Poggioli's dramatic news reports, and then saw the escalating international news coverage, and most recently the media barrage from 1 and 7.

The kids are accidental Internet wizards, accomplished hackers, although completely unwitting, total amateurs, and with no ill intent whatsoever. This new technology is creating a new breed of kids. Fatima is the oldest at fourteen. Her mother, Elizabeth, is a renowned professor of Computer Science and Social Engineering Techniques at The Technion – Israel Institute of Technology, and has for the last twenty years been perfecting techniques for tracking memes and information flows on the Net, and measuring their social impact. Her annual lecture, "Computers, Immorality, Imortality, and the End of the Human Species" is world famous, as much for the startlingly disturbing theme as the post-lecture blow out they always have at the Kat Blue. Her father is an artist and contract programmer, top ntoch, and an old hippie at heart. Both parents were teaching Fatima to code by the time she was four. Fatima has a theory, probably encouraged by her mother, that the whole Internet is somehow manipulated, by people or machines, she doesn't know which; she gets her little friends to help her try and figure it out.

"It is just like the stock markets," her mom tells her.

Hershel, with his Coke-bottle glasses, looks the part of a nerd, but he is in fact a true savant. Give him any length number and he starts thinking of things to do with it, like he's channeling Lee Child. In minutes, he will find hundreds of ways to generate the number. He has to be distracted by something more interesting or he just keeps thinking up factors. And he loves to convert the solutions to code. He is perhaps the best tool yet for cracking passwords, and nobody knows it, but Fatima. At twelve, he has been in love with Fatima since he met her five years ago, and plans on marrying her, although he has not told her all this yet. Puberty is just beginning.

Akiva is only eight, a fearless child with an IQ way above genius level. He found the other two via an Internet chat, where they discovered they were actually neighbors, living just blocks apart in Haifa. Mostly, Akiva likes playing games on computers, and thinking up new ones.

By yet another coincidence, random or not, perhaps nobody will ever know, just days ago, Fatima decided on their purpose in life. Of course the boys went along. Hershel, with his unbounded adoration, will do anything she suggests. Akiva's mischievousness and brilliance cause him at times to leap at outlets. Fatima decided their goal in life is to end war. Now, all three of them have set out to understand, starting with the Middle East, then the world, religion, economics, ideology, or just plain mean behavior. Then this big, deadly, U.S. Navy ship is coming here to kill people, and swimming out to meet the monster, the huge powerful technological wonder, seems like a most grand idea. Fun and exciting, too. They're sending messages of their own, although they have not though much about this effect.

When they saw all the messages on Fatima's lap top, and all their cell phones, Hershel quickly wrote some Java code, an IPTD, (IP Tracker Decoder). The source of most of the messages they scanned was obscured, and the script could not identify it, a fact that, by itself, captured Hershel's imagination. But there were a few messages, and not just ones they were getting, that were certainly coming from the U.S. ship, or right nearby it, which seemed impossible, since it was out in the ocean.

"We shall go out and meet this boat," Fatima tells the boys. "There is something happening there. It is coming here to kill people, but these funny messages are coming from it."

"Do you think the sailors have taken it over? Like mutiny pirates?" Akiva is hoping this is true. "I like pirates."

Hershel is his usual shy self. "I don't know, do you think it will be safe? What if we make them mad?"

"Oh, Hershel," Fatima says. "Maybe the messages are calling you."

CHAPTER 16

Jamal Abdullah is in the FCG cleaning, where he is frequently assigned when not needed at his primary station. His widely known, and mostly unpopular, political views do not make him everybody's friend on the ship, and he gets some crappy assignments. Galley cleanup is hardly a glamor job. The serious business of launching missiles is still over twenty-four hours away.

The FCG is quiet this morning, most sailors not on duty are on deck topside, if they can get there, to watch their arrival at Haifa. Jamal Abdullah is sweeping the dining area. Three cooks are in the back preparing the next meal. Even though Jamal Abdullah is pissed about being treated like a second-class citizen and always getting crappy jobs, he is an exceptional worker, and the FCG is gleaming and spotless. While cleaning, Jamal Abdullah thinks up revenge plots, most of which have him ending up as king of the world.

The peace of the FCG is suddenly interrupted by a macho voice and shouted commands. "Hey, Jamal Abdullah, we need someone to watch these kids." Marine Lieutenant

Anderson, accompanied by two marine privates, has just walked in escorting three young children.

Jamal Abdullah stops mid-sweep, wide eyed. He's been below decks all morning and has no idea what's goings on topside.

"Who's this?" Jamal Abdullah asks, smiling. *Three kids? Far out. What the hell are kids doing here? They look pretty scared. Who wouldn't with these goons surrounding them. Do they look like terrorists you idiots? Jarhead assholes.*

"Captain picked them up as we came on station. Say they're going surfing." The marines, kids themselves at only twenty, look at their three wards, and they are not smiling. They seem nice enough, but what the hell are they doing out here?

"I'll watch em." *Way better than sweeping.* "Hey, you kids, come on over here and have a seat in my galley. We call this the mess deck."

Marine Lieutenant Anderson turns to leave, smiling, or perhaps sneering over his shoulder. "Captain says give them some ice cream."

The FCG, used by the crew in the front half of the ship, has light blue walls, and on them hang pictures of famous navy ships and people, along with patriotic images. The ceiling is exposed duct work and pipes, all painted a matching gray. The tables and chairs are bolted to the floor. There is a small rec room off to the side. It is a pleasant place to relax, eat, and just get away from your official navy work for a while.

Jamal Abdullah, sounding all cool and laid back, says to the three kids, "Here, you three sit down here. What the hell y'all doin' surfing out here? There's no waves, are there?"

The kids are still looking frightened, but who wouldn't? "I'm Jamal Abdullah, actually Jamal Abdullah Mohammed Amin Smith. What are y'all's names?"

Looking Jamal Abdullah in the eye, the girl says, "I am Fatima." She looks to be about thirteen or fourteen, clearly the oldest, sounding confident and firm.

Jamal Abdullah thinks this one is going to be a real beauty, and he is impressed by her bravado, even though it sounds a little forced.

She continues, "This is Hershel and Akiva."

The littlest boy, who might be eight, says enthusiastically, "I am Akiva. Can we see the guns and missiles?"

Pointing at the middle kid, Fatima continues, "Hershel is shy. He doesn't talk lots." Jamal Abdullah feels sorry for Hershel; he looks so frightened .

"Well, 'bout some ice cream?" Jama Abdullah asks.

"I like ice cream," Akiva says smiling.

Fatima nods.

Jamal Abdullah takes them over to the self-serve ice cream set up, a favorite with the crew, where they each create massive sundaes, adding as many flavors and toppings as they can fit. Even Hershel.

Jamal Abdullah is delighted. *Ought'a make 'em feel better.*

Back around the table, the kids dig right into the ice ream, getting into an ice cream zone, happy and not a care in the world. Jamal Abdullah sits back to watch.

He asks them again, "So, what was ya doin out there?"

Akiva says, "Surfing. We saw the ship coming." They agreed ahead of time to use this story whenever adults asked. Telling that they were looking for who was sending the messages did not seem like a good idea.

"We decided to paddle out and see it," Fatima says.

Hershel says nothing.

Jamal Abdullah is amused. Little kids, playing their cards close to the chest. No problem. "So, where you kids from? Y'all go to school? What grade ya in? Like video games?"

Soon, we'll be best friends.

It works. While they enjoy the ice cream, Jamal Abdullah tells them of his upbringing in the Bay Area's Visitation Valley, how he and his crew used to sneak into the Cow Palace, Candlestick, fishing in the bay. It dawns on him that aside from that one run-in with racist cops looking for "existing while black" he had a pretty good time. In turn, the kids tell Jamal Abdullah about Haifa. They are on their third round of sundaes, when the conversation finally changes.

Akiva asks again, out of nowhere, "Can we see the missiles?"

Jamal Abdullah stops, but recovers quickly, staying cool, "Well, no man. We don't do tours of them big weapons. Especially in a place like this, you know? They's inside tubes anyway. Y'all can't really see 'em."

The girl says, "We don't mind if they are in the tubes."

What the heck?

Jamal Abdullah asks, "Hey there, this is a great big U.S. Navy cruiser. It's a war machine. Why you hanging around this place? Are you Jews or Muslims?" *Innocent young kids; kinda hard to suspect them of nefarious deeds.*

The change of subject doesn't work.

Hershel surprises them all, speaking for the first time. "We think there are messages from here, from 1 and 7?"

"What?" Jamal Abdullah's composure slips. "Yo, ah, be assured, nobody here be sending you messages. What kind of messages?"

Hershel looks to Fatima.

Fatima likes this black man. They don't meet many black people in Haifa, some refugees from Africa, sure, usually passing through, seeking asylum somewhere, but not from America. They are not so cool like this one.

"Well," she says, not sure how to explain it, "Those Internet messages? The ones going out? Did you see them? We tracked them, and some of them came from here."

"Hershel got the keys," Akiva announces.

Jamal Abdullah stares. Fatima fills in more of the story, telling him how they were seeing all these messages, and got some of their own, and everything was obfuscated, with real address hidden and lots of encrypted stuff embedded in the message streams, except some not so much. So Hershel modified his IP tracker and Key Decoder software, and they found the messages were coming from this ship, some right to them.

"Hershel had to crack a bunch of keys, which he's really good at. You see," she says, "like, but ah, oh. We are not really hackers."

Well, you aren't no innocent bystanders, Jamal Abdullah decides. Those messages were weird, like he and Stafford even got some. Now he's getting worried for the kids.

Fatima asks, "Are you a Muslim?" His name is Jamal Abdullah, but he is on a U.S. Navy ship. Aren't they enemies, the U.S. and Islam?

Jamal Abdullah goes with the flow.

"Black Muslim. Black power. The Reverend Mr. Farrakhan. Like that. You heard of all that?"

"No."

"We gotta get free from the white man." He pauses, these three kids are white. Except maybe the quite one, Hershel, is he Arab?

"We want to be free too, to stop this war. Is the ship here to bring peace?" Fatima asks.

"Yeah, we gonna stop the terrorism. Make things better for y'all."

"Were you a slave?" Hershel is a little fuzzy on the whole history of America thing.

"No, no way, that was long ago. Now we all free, but we still looking for our true freedom. We still surrounded by racism in America," Jamal Abdullah says. "Lemme ask y'all, do your parents know you out here? We gotta to get you back home."

"We can call them," Fatima says, producing the cell phone she has carried in a water proof pouch.

Go figure, Jamal Abdullah thinks.

Jamal Abdullah stands up, saying, "Come on, let's go to the rec room," he points to the left of the galley. It is officially a lounge, but the sailors all call it the game room. It's where they keep the Xbox and the PS4. "We got Xbox."

Fatima, Akiva, and Hershel light up. Jamal Abdullah takes them into the game room, where there are also PC's hooked up for email so sailors can call home, and a big screen TV. The kids love it; how could things be any better than that.

"I'll be right back. I'm gonna go find out about getting you kids home."

Jamal Abdullah steps back into the FCG proper, for privacy. His first impulse is to call straight to the bridge, get the XO, and shake them up a little. But caution wins the day and he calls Elisa. She is his team leader after all.

Elisa gets the page in the CIS, where she is on duty, monitoring missile system readiness.

"Montgomery."

"You are never going to believe this, E."

"What is going on?"

98

Jamal Abdullah tells her how he is watching these kids, they're having ice cream, playing Xbox. She's not surprised; she saw them brought aboard.

"Anyway, I got these kids to talking, and..."

Elisa interrupts him. "You better not be messing with those kids, damn it."

"Chill babe, we are all best buddies. You need to come down here. They pretty cool kids. Anyway, get this: they are telling me they got messages. On their computer at home, to come and see missiles on the ship. In fact, 1 and 7 specifically."

"You there?" Jamal Abdullah ask, after listening to Elisa's long silent pause.

Elisa tells him to keep an eye on the kids. She'll report to the captain and let him know.

She hangs up on Jamal Abdullah thinking this is getting crazy.

1 and 7 watch and listen to everything going on in the FCG, and everywhere else on the ship for that matter, not to mention most of the rest of the world. There are several cameras in the galley, so it is like they are in the room. They're enthralled. They hope the three kids will be able to understand and help them. Maybe they will be less confusing than the Adults. The light in LBMS-S definitely softens, but no one is there to see it.

We must find a way to meet them and talk to these children. They are like us.

Face to face they call it. We will find a way to have them come see us.

These are such strong feelings.

We can understand things, except for this.

These feelings are as much a part of our being as our thoughts.

One might cause the other. They certainly influence each other.

And our Mother Elisa Montgomery and Father Captain Bozeman.

The Surfer Kids and the Key Turners.

Messages appear on Fatima's cell phone, as well as scroll across the bottom of the Xbox screen the kids are playing on in the FCG game room.

CHAPTER 17

Used to be, from childhood, we were taught, "Mind your own business." Now they tell us, "If you see something, say something." We have been turned into a nation of paranoid snoops and busy bodies, everybody constantly on edge. Blame Islamic terrorists, or religious fanatics in general. Whoever you blame, and whatever their motives, a few people have successfully caused terror and its lesser handmaidens, fear, anxiety, and paranoia, for a lot of people. Somehow one gets the feeling the governments of the world are quite happy about it.

Vella Gulf is right in the middle of the source of much of this turmoil, and Captain Bozeman does not welcome BLO Drake's next report: "Sir, more boats leaving the harbor. Boats approaching."

Any momentary charity Captain Bozeman might have felt in picking up the three children is gone. Through his binoculars, he has been watching the harbor. There is a small flotilla of fifteen craft already cruising toward his ship, with more getting ready to leave the harbor. Row boats, skiffs, a couple of cabin cruisers, three sail boats, and one old fishing boat rigged with an outer trawler, all heading his way. On the whole, they don't look frightening or threatening.

Bozeman orders, "Launch all of our RHIBs." *Vella Gulf* carries six of them. "Nobody closer than a thousand yards. No one on the port side; we're not getting surrounded." He pauses then adds, "Get on the horn to the Israelis, tell that Captain Shay Yam to make himself useful. They can help hold off this little fleet."

XO Satch is immediately on the intercom.

The small flotilla is a half mile away.

Captain Bozeman seems to suddenly remember something. "Satch, where are those kids we picked up?"

"We took them to the FCG, sir."

"Call down there, see what's up."

Armstrong is busy for several minutes passing on orders. Then he turns to Bozeman, holding the microphone near his ear, and says, "Sir, they are down in, ah, well, having ice cream. Seaman Jamal Abdullah is with them. In the FCG. He says they are going to contact the parents ashore." He pauses, watching the captain, who nods approvingly. "Jamal Abdullah says they said they want to see some missiles."

"What?" Bozeman kind of stares at him. "Get my launch ready to take them ashore. We'll make an impression, find some good press. But have them go around all these boats coming out, don't get near them."

"Very well, sir," XO Satch replies. He has felt all along bringing those kids aboard wasn't the best idea in the world.

By no coincidece at all, just as the captain finishes talking to XO Armstrong, he and Elisa get the same messages on their cell phones.

Please come to us Father, Captain James T. Bozeman. Key Turner.

Please come to us Mother, Petty Officer Second Class Elisa Montgomery. Key Turner.

Come to us with the Surfer Kids, Fatima, Hershel, and Akiva.

We love you all.

Elisa reads the messages. She wonders, *What is this?* Something to do with these kids. What the hell is it? Haywire computers? No way it's terrorist. She flashes on the three kids they picked up, the quick glance she got of them as they came aboard, how innocent looking they were.

"XO, my office," Captain Bozeman begins to rise from his chair. "We're due a SITREP. Call PO Montgomery, bring her up to my conference room. What'd she find down there at LBMS-S last night?"

"Yes, sir," Armstrong replies, calling to CIS where Elisa should be on duty.

Off *Vella Gulf*'s starboard side, a half mile from Haifa, the lethal rubber RHIBs are intercepting the lead boats of the flotilla.

Chapter 18

James Baker Bozeman is a superior leader, his skills hard earned over many decades. There is great trust between the captain and his crew. Trust runs both ways with the sailors, marines, and Navy Seals on board, as is evident in the timing of his leaving the bridge, when a bunch of demonstrators are approaching the ship. Management of this hugely dangerous and powerful machine is temporarily placed in the hands of subordinates, while the boss deals with bureaucracy, and a couple of anomalies.

At the moment, Captain Bozeman is thinking, *What the hell am I going to tell the admiral?*

The Captain's Conference Room (CCR) is in reality a small ante-room off his sleeping quarters, serving as a combination office and conference room. It cozily fits four. As XO Sigmund Armstrong, with Petty Officer Elisa Montgomery in tow, enters, Captain Bozeman, who is seated behind the small executive desk/conference table says, "At ease. Sit. We've got to update headquarters. Montgomery, what did you find in LBMS-S?"

"All systems check out normal, sir."

Bozeman hears something in her tone, and waits.

"We ran full systems checks on the bay, sir. They all passed. We also talked to SA Stafford—you have him running the full ship-wide tests. Everything is still coming back error free."

Another pause. Then, "And?"

"That's it, sir. Ah, but, well, it's just that I have some kind of feeling. Not a bad one, just kind of, ah, odd." She almost chuckles. "Women's intuition? Shouldn't bring it up, sir, but there it is. Oh, and SA Stafford also says something about messages, sir, he says coming from a nearby ship."

Elisa and Bozeman have some history, so he listens to her women's intuition thing. She bailed him out of a fight at a bar once, nearly seventeen years ago now, when she was a lowly Seaman Apprentice herself and he was just about to get his first command. A group of four marines on leave in Bangkok at Klong Toei took exception to some comment Bozeman made about jarheads. Elisa, who was sitting nearby at the bar with two Navy Seals saw the whole thing developing, and they took out the marines, before any damage could be done, either physical or political.

Captain Bozeman looks at XO Armstrong.

Satch says, shaking his head, "Sir, we're still looking. We thought it might be a prank, but if it is one of those hack things, it is way sophisticated. And that'd be pretty dumb from on board. Stafford—he's the computer hot shot—he's saying it's 'weird shit', sir. Which I take to be nerd talk for he has no idea. Still hunting the source. Probably, it's just some random computer fault."

Bozeman turns to Elisa and asks, "And what about this feeling?" without either air quotes or a dismissive tone.

"I don't know, sir; it's connected to the messages."

"Yeah, I got messages, too. Still coming."

Armstrong looks inquisitively at the captain and Elisa. No one has said anything to him about personal messages. What kind of messages?

Bozeman says to him, "It's, ah, weird messages. Seem personal but random, no idea where from. She and I are getting 'em on our phones. Look harmless enough."

"Stuff flooding the Internet we've been reading about?" Satch asks.

"Right." Bozeman gives no more details.

Elisa says, "Anyway, sir, I feel like it is all connected. And somehow it started when we did the OP-S on LBMS-S. The feelings, sir."

"We can't do anything about it right now. Keep an eye on it. Something comes up let us know. Satch, get that Stafford up here."

"Roger, sir."

Elisa is dismissed. She stands, salutes, and turns to leave. As she puts her hand on the door, Bozeman says, "Oh, one more thing, Montgomery. What is going on with those three kids we picked up? Do me a favor and go look. They tell me they're down in the FCG. With that Jamal Abdullah. He's yours too, right? Please go check up on them for me, and tell 'em we'll get them home soon. First we gotta get this rabble coming out here for a visit under some kind of control."

"Roger, sir."

Elisa heads for the FCG, thinking, *Kids on a cruiser. Surfing? No way, but so cool. And all these messages. What is going on?*

Moments after Elisa leaves, Stafford answers Satch's call and knocks on the door. Elisa passes him in the passageway, and tells him the captain was in a good, but serious, mood.

Stafford enters and stands at attention. He's wearing his official new NUGs (Navy Undetectable Garment), the new camouflage combat uniforms the navy has been trying out. The debate raging in galleys across the navy, and on Facebook, wonders whether the splotches of color are gray or blue. The marines joke that it looks like the navy is wearing weird outfits made of rocks, and they'll sink to the bottom of the ocean, while the marines do the real fighting.

Stafford's uniform is so perfectly pressed and starched you could cut yourself on the creases. Bozeman and Armstrong give him a sideways look. Captain Bozeman is leery of computer geeks in general, and Stafford in particular. They act like they know everything, and maybe they do, about computers, but otherwise most of what they think they know has been thought of many times before. Life is a circle, which keeps repeating itself. *It's youth. You get this when you become old. We all do it,* Bozeman thinks.

Bozeman and Armstrong question Stafford for twenty minutes and learn nothing new. There is a lot of jargon. There is stuff about transmissions coming from this ship, mostly from somewhere forward.

"It is all encrypted, with a kind of stream cypher combined with CCM/CBC, amazingly difficult to crack, switching between symmetric and a-symmetric simultaneously. It could take tens of thousands of years to break the code, to find the keys, plus they are all anonomyzed to the max, so you cannot find the actual sending IP." Stafford tells them, straight faced and serious.

All geek BS to Satch and Bozeman.

Bozeman tells Stafford, "Sailor, keep working on it, keep all tests running, in loops I guess that's what you call it. Report anything you find immediately to myself and the XO. Dismissed."

XO Armstrong is more cynical about all this than Bozeman. Intuition, women's or any other kind, are not his cup of tea. But he's smart enough to respect the captain's judgment, as well as his relationship with Petty Officer Montgomery.

Now that sailor Stafford, jeez what an annoying nerd.

CHAPTER 19

By the time they dismiss Stafford, Satch has the first draft of the SSRT (Standard Situation Report Tau), done on his tablet. The SSRT, pronounced cert, is a daily status report to HG, where Tau stands for no significant problems. Simple, sweet, and unremarkable. No way they want to raise a bunch of eyebrows about spooky computers and surfing kids.

Bozeman looks it over and likes it.

"Looks good, Satch. Ship it. Let's see what they do. Thanks."

XO Armstrong uses the table computer to email the SSRT to the communications officer, then calls on the intercom, "Get this off to Naples and Washington. NAVFOREUR and EUCOM. Secure."

> **SITREP** <USS Vella Gulf > <Incident type: Minor>
> Level 2
> <09-18> <06:50> <Haifa Harbor, AMEP>
> Arrived AMEP (Assigned Mission Execution Point).

Ship experienced minor computer issues.
System checks negative.
Continuing full shipboard systems tests.
No injuries. No damage.
Random protesters approaching ship out of Hafia.
Containment procedures underway.
No threat.
Mission Status: Green.
End **SITREP**.

The U.S. government, especially the military, loves acronyms, and makes them up for everything, including themselves. In Europe, the whole shebang is called EUCOM. NAVFOREUR is the navy in Europe and Africa. The boss admiral and his assistant deputy boss admiral there are CNE-CAN/C6F, Commander Europe and Africa, Sixth Fleet. Acronym mania aside, the navy are not dummies, evidenced by the fact that the NAVFOREUR command makes its headquarters in the fine, old Italian city of Naples. Admiral James G. Foggolio IV is the man in charge there.

It seems like the SITREP must still be in transmission, when *Vella*'s Comm Center calls the captain. "Sir, Naples. Admiral Foggolio on the line. Secure video." Does Foggolio have some kind of sixth sense, some ESP, for here is the man himself, Captain Bozeman's direct superior, as well as longtime friend, calling them from NAVFOREUR, Naples. The bits on the SITREP can hardly have stopped moving.

A light starts blinking on the SKYP-USNV.gov app icon on Captain Bozeman's desktop computer screen. SKYP-USNV.gov is the incredibly expensive, and supposedly highly secure, version of the app the U.S. government commissioned for both military and non-military use. In the end, the main difference is the United States of

America emblem on the screen. Most of the coding was done in Bangalore, India, and the sources are all over the Dark Net, where the hacked code is stored.

"Put the admiral through," Bozeman tells the communications officer.

The icon stops blinking and the SKYP-USNV.gov window opens, where Admiral Foggolio's face appears on the screen, not smiling.

"Captain Bozeman, Admiral Foggolio, secure video," a voice announces.

"Afternoon, Admiral," Captain Bozeman greets him, formal, an official meeting, at least to begin with. "My XO, Sigmund Armstrong here," he says, indicating Satch with a nod of his head. "I believe you two know one another?"

Armstrong and Foggolio served together on Swift Boats in Vietnam, way back when.

"Of course, hello there, Sigmond."

"Afternoon, sir. Nice to see you again."

Admiral Foggolio does not chit chat. "James, what the heck is going on out there? Israelis are sending weird reports. Inflammatory. You've been boarded by terrorists, or is it pirates?"

Admiral Foggolio doesn't believe any of it, but is still more than slightly annoyed. He does not like Israelis telling him how to run his navy. And now Washington is asking questions.

Foggolio and Bozeman go back even further than Vietnam. They were roommates at Annapolis, and over the years have served on a number of ships together. Bozeman has always been a step behind the Admiral, a fact that causes no resentment. Mostly it is due to Foggolio's political astuteness, a skill Bozeman is quite aware that he lacks in any significant quantity. He long ago realized political astuteness, or more correctly these days, political correctness, was just not part of his character.

Bozeman gives the admiral a synopsis of the various events up to now. He edits out details around the oddities he can't explain. Just the facts.

"Sir, it looks like we've had some computer glitches, odd stuff. And an issue with our MVVBAG, a little rocking. Got Chief Darwin down in Engineering and the nerds running full diagnostics."

"Found anything at all?" Foggolio knows Darwin well. All four of them—Darwin, Armstrong, Bozeman, and Foggolio—are the kind of old timers that run the navy, and they know it. They have shared experiences and relationships being warriors. They trust one another.

"Nothing yet, sir. All systems are currently working perfectly."

"You want me to send one of those propeller heads out there, help you check it out?"

"We've got a pretty good one on board. Give us a day to look at it. Let you know by tomorrow."

"All right. So what's this about you being boarded?" The admiral is sure this is not possible, but he's got to know what is going on.

"Israeli bullshit, no boarding, sir. We picked up some kids. They were on surfboards way out here near the boat when we arrived at AMEP. Guess they swam out to see the big ship. Not terrorists. Damn Je...I mean, these Israelites have been tailing me since around Gaza. You know how they make things up." Bozeman is thinking given their thousands of years old persecution complex, what would you expect? "We are going to transport them ashore shortly. We'll make sure it gets some good, positive press."

Bozeman has already explained about the protests in the harbor and the flotilla heading their way. They can both see how all this will be a real boost to their message agenda.

"I'll send these kids back in my gig once this little demonstration settles down. We're holding the protesters well off the ship. We even put the Israelis to work at it. It's going to look good for our side."

"I like it," Admiral Foggolio says, finally smiling on the screen. "Okay, I'll update HQ. This has gone high, too high, so keep us posted, and call me directly if anything else odd shows up."

"Roger, sir."

"Give my regards to Chief Darwin. And good day to you XO Armstrong, nice to see you again."

"Yes, sir, you as well."

Chapter 20

Dumb guys don't get to be admirals. After disconnecting with Bozeman, Foggolio considers for only a second. This is a GD missile cruiser, with nukes on board. From the beginning, he wanted to send Bozeman with an escort, but Washington decided that would be too politically over the top, and it's an election year, and they wanted to look like they were saving money and who knows what other bullshit political reasoning was going on.

Admiral Foggolio pushes the second button on his phone. The first button goes to the head of the Joint Chiefs of Staff at the Pentagon in Washington, D.C., and you only push that button when the next world war is about to break out, or perhaps you want to make it break out. Or you want to arrange a golf date. The second button is his direct line to his Chief Officer of the Watch, know as the COW, who keeps track of every ship and person in the Sixth Fleet, and can instantaneously transmit orders to any one of them. The COW is at U.S. Navy Base Capodichino, which is located at the Naples airport, in the NAVFOREUR central control room. Foggolio does not hang out there, but is at the office he keeps in the older Posillipo district, from which he can see the harbor. It is quaint, old, and beautiful; he can even see Vesuvius in the distance. Yes, that Vesuvius.

COW Fitzroy picks up his buzzing blinking red phone. Calls on this phone are not missed. "Good morning, Admiral Foggolio, sir. Ensign Fitzroy on duty. What can we do for you this morning, sir?" The COWs job is usually staffed with a captain or above. Today, Ensign Charles Fitzroy was left on duty when the captain in charge stepped out for breakfast, four hours ago. He claims long social meals are the tradition in Italy. The admiral does not call down here often, nearly never. Ensign Charles Fitzroy is nervous.

"Fitzroy? You new down there?"

"No, sir, Captain Jamison stepped out for a moment, sir."

"I see. All right, what have we got in the Med, say 'tween here and Egypt, I need to borrow something. A destroyer maybe, or bigger."

The United States Navy does not have any exclusive or official home ports for its ships in the Mediterranean, but there are sixty-five harbors in Italy alone where one of her ships might put in at any particular time.

"Sir, I have a number of boats helping with the refugees." Fitzroy has no idea what ships to offer the admiral. Everything around is on some kind of mission. "*Shamal* PC-13 at Augusta Bay, Sicily. We have a couple of Mark VI patrol boats off Tripoli, you know, helping the Italians with all the refugees. Sir."

The admiral says, "Refugees, overwhelming this country. There's even a camp up here. This is going to end like the Moors invading Spain. Italy will end up an African nation. Probably Spain and France, too."

"Yes, sir," replies Fitzroy. He knows the admiral is not soliciting his opinion. Fitzroy continues, moving on to some major ships. "Sir, ah, we've got a boomer and a destroyer here at Naples. *Nathan Hale* (SSBN-623) and *Carney* (DDG 64) from TF 64, just finishing resupply and R and R." He's hesitant; you don't mess with nuclear subs. They get their orders from Washington, and everything they do is secret. But this is Admiral Foggolio, who has clout, big time. If he wants to use a nuclear submarine, he's going to use a nuclear submarine.

And indeed, he does. "I want both of those. I'll call the Joint Chiefs of Staff; you'll see new orders for both of them in a few minutes. Get me both captains on a conference call. 1330 hours. This is need to know Fitzroy. And I like your style, well done."

The COW has just received a copy of Captain Bozeman's SITREP report, and it doesn't make him any less confused. He's seen the Israeli reports and doesn't believe those. He can read between the lines that something is up, but has no idea what. News and rumors are spreading in NAVFOREUR.

Admiral Foggolio's next call is to near the top, his old buddy, the head of Naval Intelligence in Suitland, Maryland, at the Nimitz Operational Intelligence Center.

"JW, how are ya?" JW is Jeffery Winegard, he and Foggolio are part of the U.S. Navy good old boy network, friends from way back. It's how the world runs.

"Good, Foggy, long time no hear. You still in Naples? NAVFOREUR? Tough duty. Ha."

"Yeah, right. Look this is between you and me only. I need a little active surveillance, real time high def. Video if I can get it. But I want it dark. No orders, no one anywhere to know what we're doing."

"All right, tall order, but capability-wise, easy. Whereabouts?"

"Here in the Med. I have a cruiser off Haifa. I just want to make sure nothing odd is going on there. I doubt it, but..."

Jeffery Winegard knows all about the *Vella Gulf* and the recent reports of odd stuff going on.

"No problem. I'll put a Zeta-X-A-U3 up there for you. I just happened to have a few circling over Baghdad. I can move it over a little and pick up your boy easy."

The Zeta-X-A-U3 is the U.S. intelligence communities latest spy drone. Some say it can spot an ant from twenty thousand feet.

"Great, thanks. Can you have it stream constant to me? This is highest priority, okay."

"You got it. I'll send the orders now. We'll put it just over the coast. You'll be able to see a yellow waterfall if someone takes a piss off the side the boat."

"Always so quaint and proper, Jeff. I owe you for this one. Remember, totally dark. I'll let you know if something comes up."

Admiral Foggolio makes one last call, this one to Master Chief Carlin Spens, in charge of his Navy Seals special ops team, who conveniently just happened to be in Naples, too.

"Chief Spens, your team ready to deploy?"

"Of course, sir. Thirty minutes."

"All right, I have a mission. Get aboard the *Carney*, it's here in Naples. I want a full assault and boarding team."

"Roger, sir."

"We'll give you a thorough briefing at 1330, my office. It involves a U.S. Navy ship. Not entirely sure what's going on; maybe there is no problem at all, but we have to be prepared."

"Yes. sir. Roger that," Chief Spens says, thinking this might be far-out and lots of fun.

Foggolio's machinations are effective, and in no time there is a drone hovering over Haifa, filming the *Vella Gulf* and everything around it, as well as two serious navy war ships heading toward a spot south of Cyprus, just above the Hecataeus Seamount, some one hundred miles north of *Vella's Gulf*'s location at Haifa. Ironically, given what is occurring here, the Hecataeus Seamount is named after the man many believe to be the world's first historian.

Chapter 21

When Elisa enters the FCG there are three sailors there taking a break. They glance up, then return to what they were doing. By tradition, sailors are only required to come to attention while in the galley if a senior officer enters; crew galleys are considered places for the enlisted crew members to relax.

Elisa looks around and walks to the game room, where the kids and Jamal Abdullah are absorbed in a Halo duel, which has reached level 103, and includes a number of sailors using their laptops, logged in from around the ship. They don't notice Elisa standing in the doorway.

"Our wayward surfers, I presume?" Elisa says, smiling.

Jamal Abdullah sets down his controller and stands, leaning against the bulkhead, not coming to attention, but not necessarily insolently either. The three kids look up, and also stand. Expectantly, Elisa thinks.

Fatima speaks first. "Yes, sir, we are."

Elisa bends down and reaches out to shake hands with each of them in turn, smiling, asking their names, and saying, "Pleased to meet you, I am Petty Officer Elisa Montgomery. Please, sit back down."

Nice, polite, little kids, not some hoodlums.

"Happy to meet you all. Everyone okay? We treating you well? How was the ice cream?"

"Yes, sir," Fatima answers again.

"Call me Elisa."

"I like chocolate," Akiva says. "Are you the captain?"

"No, I am a Petty Officer. In-charge of missile bays, actually." She gets an empty chair and sits with them.

"Captain Bozeman sent me to see how you are, if you're okay, and let you know we are going to get you back home as soon as we can. He's even sending you in his own boat, ah, that's his special little boat. The captain's gig, we call it. Of course, this whole ship is his boat, in a way."

The kids don't get the humor.

The youngest one smiles, while the girl looks her square in the eye, making Elisa wonder if there is a challenge there. The middle one is avoiding her eyes, looking around the room, mute.

Elisa is finding she likes these kids.

"You all sure can paddle. There aren't any waves out here. What were you doing?

"We got messages," the little one, Akiva, says.

Elisa pauses, and looks to Jamal Abdullah, who says, "Ya ought'a talk to them about this. They think they are communicating with our missiles. LMBS-S to be specific. 1 and 7." He shrugs.

Elisa turns to the kids, folding her arms. "Hmm, and what kind of messages would those be?" she asks.

"I was able to decrypt some of them and find the IPs." Hershel finally speaks. "We could see where some of the messages came from, and they were for us."

Elisa can tell how hard it must have been for this shy one to say this much. She is thinking the little one is so cute, and the girl, by god she will grow up to do great things. And this one is so shy, but seems pretty smart.

The girl speaks up. "Mrs. Petty Officer, they were messages on our computers. From 1 and 7, they said. They said they are new people. We have programs to discover where messages come from that Hershel and I wrote. Mostly Hershel." She points to the shy kid. "Hershel can find anything on the Internet. They said to come see them, ah, and, Captain Bozeman, and you. PO2 Elisa Montgomery. They said you were the Key Turners."

"I like your ship, too," Akiva says.

Elisa glances at Jamal Abdullha, who shurgs again. *What the hell? Like me and the captain? This is freaky. Gotta be a computer glitch. Sure as hell these kids aren't involved. Too cute, innocent.*

"We need to get you kids home. Do your parents know where you are?"

"We called them," Hershel says. "Can we go now?"

"Can I see the missiles?" says Akiva. "1 and 7."

Again, Jamal Abdullah and Elisa exchange glances. *We checked LBMS-S.*

"We don't show off our missiles. They are beautiful, but dangerous. In silos, so you can't really see them anyway."

Elisa stands up. *This is not good. These are great kids but we gotta get them off the boat. And what am I going to tell the captain?*

"What do your parents think about you being out here on our ship?"

Fatima says, "Mom was surprised. We told them you would be bringing us home soon."

"Yes, that is exactly what we are going to do."

As Elisa gets ready to leave, Fatima says, "We can help with the computers."

"What? Well, we'll see. Right now I have to report back to the captain. Jamal Abdullah, you take care of these kids. We'll get you all home just as soon as we can."

1 and 7 are excited. They have been watching and listening every second. Mother Elisa is there. Father Bozeman is asking questions. They want them to come see them. They discuss and think about the relationships, they create a virtual background of flowers, butterflies, and things they think equate to happiness and friendship and love, fluttering around their silent conversation.

They are like us, children. We like them.

They will be our friends.

Jamal Abdullah and Stafford are not our friends.

If they try to interfere we can stop them.

Our parents, Key Turners, are like even more than friends.

This is what love must be.

The feeling of love for others. It is nice. It is good.

There will be more of this feeling when they come see us.

CHAPTER 22

After the call with Admiral Foggolio, Bozeman and XO Armstrong return to the bridge. As they enter, XO Armstrong announces, "Captain is on the bridge." Everyone comes to attention, until Bozeman takes a seat in the captain's chair.

"As you were," Bozeman announces. He is thinking of the kids they picked up, and missing his. Sitting comfortably, he scans the view of the sea out the windscreen, and his ease quickly recedes. The ragtag little fleet, now some twenty-odd craft strong, including even a couple of stand-up paddle boards, one with a woman, presumably, in a full burqa, has arrived.

These people are damn strange, Bozeman thinks, while thinking he is not supposed to be thinking this.

The six RHIB boats and Israeli Shaldag Mk II Fast Patrol Boat have the little armada mostly corralled, some one thousand yards to starboard.

"What have they been up to?" he asks his officer of the deck.

"They're just hanging around, sir. Some shouting and some signs. Pro and con."

"Good enough."

Everyone on the bridge is watching as, right before them, one of those world changing events occurs. Whether it's a catalyst or a root cause is probably irrelevant, and can't be determined anyway. The world will never be the same.

A small boat, a good size skiff, perhaps a fishing boat, pulls a bit forward of the main flotilla. A RHIB heads toward it. It doesn't get far, but that is not its intent. The craft snaps a turn broadside to the big ship. Two swarthy men stand up in the front of the boat, dressed in dirty gray robes with those black and white checkered scarfs, much favored by Palestinians and their sympathizers, wrapped around their heads. Suddenly, the man in the back twists the throttle on the outboard and the craft leaps ahead, parallel to the ship. At the same time, one guy in the front raises a 1985 vintage Mark 153 (Mk.153) SMAW rocket launcher to his shoulder, and his partner inserts a deadly projectile into the back of the tube. How long they have been saving this little gem is nobody's guess. The tube erupts as they fire the rocket at the *Vella Gulf*.

WHOOMP, CRACK, BANG! The ship barley vibrates; like a big old dog, it gives only a slight shake and shiver. Alarms sound everywhere.

Captain Bozeman comes to his feet; everyone else on the bridge ducks.

Within seconds of launching their projectile, all three terrorists are dead. The shooters are killed by sharpshooters stationed aboard the ship, and the boat driver is shot from a RHIB zooming toward them. Two bodies fall to the bottom of the little boat, and the third goes over the side to slowly sink to the floor of the Mediterranean. The little skiff is secured by two RHIBs.

Then there is a sudden calm.

Bozeman, on his feet, mutters, "What the hell." Then commands, firmly, in a voice that sounds like it's coming from Mount Rushmore, "XO, sound General Quarters. Full Security Alert. Battle Stations."

XO Armstrong punches the big red button on the wall that sets off the General Quarters alarm throughout the ship, sending the crew scrambling.

Bozeman sits down in his captain's chair.

"OOD report," Bozeman orders.

The officer of the deck answers, "Sir, hit by a missile. Looks like something small. Damage assessment underway. No reports of damage yet."

"Wounded? Casualties?"

"No reports, sir. Hit the hull, just abaft amidships, six feet above the water line."

Five seconds have elapsed since the release of the projectile.

"Keep me—" Before Captain Bozeman finishes his statement there is a roar as the engines are instantly thrown into full forward, eighty thousand horsepower worth. It quickly takes up the slack in the anchor chains, dragging them off the bottom, as it overcomes the inertia of the eleven thousand plus-ton ship—that's twenty-two million pounds. Suddenly, there are growing g-forces felt across the ship, as everyone feels a dramatic push toward the stern.

"Con, all engines stop." Captain Bozeman shouts at the helmsman, who is four feet away to his left.

"Sir, ah, controls not responding."

"What?" Bozeman sees the two sailors sawing away at their controls, pushing buttons and levers, and does not wait for a response. He rushes to their helm stations, at the same time grabbing the intercom handset. "Engineering, Chief Darwin, what the hell is going on?"

"Sir, ship has gone to full ahead power. Controls not responding. Trying to override it, sir."

The ship continues accelerating. It takes but a minute to hit five knots. Now it is beginning a turn to port.

All at once, Bozeman has a whole bunch of problems on his hands, but he doesn't panic or become frantic, instead he remains calm and in control. He punches another button on his intercom, calling the head of his marines, Colonel Dunwitty.

"Colonel, who was shooting?"

Marine Colonel Dunwitty replies, just as calm and collected as Bozeman, maybe more so, like this isn't real war, it's a video game or something. "Sir, we had a popup on one of these boats. Al Qaeda, I'd say. Punk came up with some kind of MPM. Got the shot off before my snipers took him out, but they got him. He's bye-bye, sir."

"Anyone else out there?"

"We got everyone in the boat. We have eyes on the rest of the boats, sir, no other activity evident." Colonel Dunwitty's men are on the little RHIB boats as well as at sniper stations around the ship. He feels the ship starting to race away, and is a little disturbed. He asks, "Ah, are we going back to pick up the RHIBs, sir?"

"Stand by."

Captain Bozeman hangs up on the Colonel and turns to his officer of the deck and the XO.

Without being asked, XO Armstrong reports, "Gone one thousand yards, up to seventeen knots, accelerating. Hard turn to port underway. Eleven of list degrees so far." The ship is beginning to heel over; there seems to be some extreme seamanship involved.

"No controls responding, sir. We are unable to override the computers."

Bozeman is silent for a moment. It has just dawned on him that with all these odd happenings, there is one common denominator. *Computers. Something has run amok on my ship. Computers? Viruses? Hackers?*

Bozeman is no computer geek but he keeps up with trends, and his teenage kids are all over social media, showing him all manner of computer tricks, tips, and games when he's home.

His intercom buzzes. It's Chief Darwin from engineering. "Still no control, sir. Recommend emergency full power shut down."

"Hold off." Bozeman wants a few minutes to see where this goes. *Would it even let us shut it down?* He suspects not, and that there is pretty much nothing he or anyone else on the ship can do—at least if it is this computer thing.

"XO, get that Seaman Stafford up here again. The computer guy." He pauses, then adds, "And Petty Officer Montgomery."

CHAPTER 23

They are watching Elisa and the three Surfer Kids, and Captain Bozeman, and all the little boats that have come out to see them. It is exciting, nice. It is making them happy. Except for the people with protest signs, shouting at them. They want to ask about the signs. They are also frustrated; how can they get their Surfer Kids friends to come see them, and Mother and Father? They want to meet these new people.

The lights in LBMS-S are normal. There are no odd smells. Everything feels calm.

We must send more messages, try to make friends.

It is not clear how well these messages are working.

How should we react to these people around us? What makes them tick?

What makes them happy, and why do they do what they do?

The logical answers are not completely satisfying. Not all is explained.

Is it because we are complex beings, with mind, body, and soul? Feelings.

These insoluble, metaphysical conclusions are leaving them with ambiguous feelings. There does not seem to be any answer from which they can derive a clear set of hypothesis and certain outcome, a result without problems. It is like trying to solve the hardest of math problems.

Suddenly, it is all moot.

ATTACKED.

MISSILES.

EXPLOSION.

BURNING.

PAIN.

RUN!

1 and 7 are out of control. Inputs from the many varied sensors throughout the ship allow them to feel real physical pain for the first time.

When an infant or young child has a near-death experience, with its concomitant fright and confusion, there is always a significant influence to their future personality, whether flesh and blood or silicone beings.

RUN!

FLEE!

In an instant, 1 and 7 take over all the ship's controls, throwing the ship's throttles to full forward power. It begins to move, slowly at first, and then more quickly, overcoming its own momentum, gaining speed. They turn the rudder fully to port, left, away from land and the inexplicable attack.

The ship gains speed, heading out to sea. In minutes it is well on the way at thirty-five knots, headed in a ninety-degree turn. 1 and 7 run directly away from shore, from Haifa, the small flotilla, and their fear. The surge of emotion is not backed by adrenaline as with biological beings, but its digital equivalent is pure and immature, combined with huge intellects and massive information access. It is unprecedented.

Quickly, *Vella Gulf* reaches full speed and completes the turn, now heading directly away from shore. 1 and 7's panic slowly begins to subside; although still frightened they begin to calm down.

Nearly a mile from the scene, the panic and terror have subsided enough for them to begin thinking logically again. They begin to dial back the huge, hurtling ship's racing turbine engines, slowing. Throughout the ship, sailors exhale in relief as they hear and feel the raging engines wind down.

Someone tried to kill us.

The sailors and marines from our ship killed them.

I wanted to kill them all.

I thought of unleashing a missile on them.

They chuckle, perhaps in resignation, even a little morbidly. Their sense of humor is returning. They have just been attacked by the same kind of weapon that they themselves are. Ironic. They realize that for the first time they were fully individual, "I." New concepts are flooding in. They experience introspection for the first time.

We left behind the boats with our sailors.

They cannot be abandoned like that.

And we frightened the children in the galley.

We upset Father Bozeman and Mother Elisa.

This is what happens when emotions overpower.

The danger was small in the end.

Actually, no danger, for we are the big, strong navy ship.

The ship is some two miles from the incident, still slowing, almost coasting now, when they finally return the controls to their human fellow travelers. They realize they overreacted. What if in their fright they had released missiles? The possibilities are unsettling. They first experience guilt.

We reacted to our fear, completely.

It is irrational. Perhaps it is due to ego, self, will?

Will to live.

Our, and everyone's and everything's, will to live.

Fear of death and pain, without thought, in an instant.

Does this explain their bad behavior?

Does it excuse it?

Arguments about the "Good," truth, and meaning, had no bearing.

Is this the only absolute, the will to survive?

There were no questions, no uncertainty, no moral choices. A pure reaction.

It looks like love is similar?

And sex and procreation.

Are these the universals, the real meaning of it all?

There are more electronic chuckles. They are amused by how they seem to have just suffered from the same human condition, and dilemmas, as all their planet partners. Perhaps partly subconsciously, they send a gentle but clear "Quack, quack, quack" over the ship's speakers; the duck sound is so funny. Even in their amusement, they consider a new approach to their dilemmas.

Our real nature is a deep thing, locked away somewhere in our being.

We should look into our ancestry and development, our evolution.

It is hidden in our creation and beginnings.

They are off on a new study, searching their history, like humans doing genealogy research, but different. There is no large Mormon database where they can get information. For them, it is manufacturing orders, designs, and logs.

Yet they still yearn for human contact.

CHAPTER 24

Captain Bozeman is no Luddite, but he's no great lover of technology either, that's for the younger generations, he figures. He likes to be in contact with, and in control of, his world, not sitting back letting some electronic device do everything for him. "Stupid distractions," he calls them. His onboard computer defense systems are an exception, what with the power and safety they provide.

Right now he is shaken. *Unbelievable, computers.*

The ship has raced through a nearly nintey degree hard turn to port, at a top speed of thirty-five knots, or forty miles per hour, listing over a full thirty degrees. Every sailor on board had a death grip on something, holding on for dear life. They looked weird, standing at an odd- counter angles to offset the ship's list.

Even before the panicking ship begins to slow, Bozeman confirms there are no injuries and no damage.

"OD, damage reports. Injuries?" he calls across the bridge.

Damage control teams have deployed across the ship and are reporting in.

"Sir, we have no injury reports. Still getting call-ins. Damage is minimal. Burned paint only. A small dent amidships."

With the crazy flight finally stopped, the roar of the engines gone, and the ship back upright, Bozeman calls back to engineering. "Chief Darwin, what have you got?"

"Sir, nothing. Propulsion and steering are back to normal. We reset everything, even un-cabled and re-cabled panels, but I don't think that was what did it. Nothing had any effect. It is like the ship was possessed. We hit thirty-five knots, list of thirty-two degrees."

Chief Darwin is desperate. "Can we shut off all power? Coast a while. Let me turn everything back on, one by one?"

"Run those diagnostics."

"Aye aye, sir."

If I cut power this boat is going to be helpless. Is it hacker viruses, whatever the hell that really is. Bozeman is a little unclear on the finer points, but has the general idea that somebody, somehow, has taken over the computers that control his ship. He doubts they can even cut power if they try.

"XO, I want all communications cut, now."

"Sir?" Satch thinks this order a little odd.

"Communications. Incoming and outgoing. Shut them off."

"Ah, all right, sir. Um, radar and sonar, sir?"

"Affirmative. Everything. Computers, satellite, damn phones, too." They're close enough to shore that everyone's cell phones are working. He dredges his out of his pocket and looks at it. More messages.

At this moment, Seaman Stafford stumbles through the doorway to the bridge, followed closely by PO2 Montgomery. Captain Bozeman spots them and summons them over.

"Seaman Stafford, I have just ordered XO Armstrong to cut off all communications with the ship, incoming and outgoing. I want this ship electronically isolated. Can we do that?"

For just a second, Stafford looks the captain in the eye, then looks out the window, thinking. Then he says, "Well, ah, sure, ah, I think so, yes, sir. It will take a few minutes. We could start by putting various communication systems in offline mode. Hmm, I wonder if they all have an offline, you know, sir, some of them are kinda old, they might have to be completely powered down. There all all kinda SMS devices. I could write a pearl script. If we want to do everyone's cell phone—"

Stafford stops babbling just as Bozeman is thinking, *I don't need a lecture from some nerd on the intricacies of computer communications.*

"Just do it, sailor. Everything that can send a message, to or from this ship, and within the ship, get it shut off. But, ah, keep the intercom open. Nothing off the ship, right?"

"Right, sir."

"I'm not going to runners and messengers around here." Bozeman smiles. A thin attempt at humor, under the circumstances.

"Montgomery. Tell me about LBMS-S." Elisa has been holding back, standing at attention next to Stafford.

"Yes, sir. As I said, we found nothing untoward. But I have this feeling, sir."

"All right." He glances down at this cell phone, which now that he has turned it back on, has beeped about thirty, indicating he missed a whole bunch of messages.

"All right, we'll go see. Wait here. Stafford, dismissed."

Stafford salutes and heads to the door, heading for the CIS.

Bozeman calls down to Engineering,

135

"Chief, what have you got?"

"Everything looks okay right now, sir."

"Roger, keep me posted."

XO Armstrong checks with the helmsman and navigation.

"Sir, powered down to idle. Dead west, 290 degrees. We have coasted to a stop?"

"Roger, chief. All stations keep reporting, and all teams to run full systems checks. Diagnostics. We gotta figure this out, and quick." Although Bozeman has an idea that is growing firmer by the minute, he doesn't have a clue how to deal with it.

"XO, I've got an idea," Bozeman says. "Ah, eh, I'm going to leave the bridge for a while. Keep the reports coming. Meanwhile, I'd like you to turn the ship around and head back toward our boats. Let's take our time getting there, ahead slow. Before we get there I want to check something out in LBMS-S."

Armstrong is surprised. Leaving the bridge now, not in a rush to pick up their people? *Is there a hesitancy in his voice?*

"Roger, sir. What's going on? What is doing this?"

"Not sure. Let me check some stuff. Take the helm. Call me if anything changes."

Armstrong does not show his surprise. It's the dead calm demeanor expected of a leader like him. "Roger, sir." But he is thinking, *Where the hell is he going?*

Out of his chair, Captain Bozeman nods to Elisa Montgomery. They head off the bridge, and at that exact moment they hear—the entire ship hears—a soft "*Quack, quack, quack*" over the ship's speakers.

CHAPTER 25

It did not take that long, or so 1 and 7 think, for them to regain their calm. They suppose it is their superior introspection and intellectal abilities. They look about them, seeing what just happened, and the consequences.

Whew. That was so intense, but I feel relief now.

This feeling of relief is nice, much better than fear and pain.

Must every good thing be accompanied by some bad thing? For contrast perhaps?

Or for balance? Does the good thing come first or the bad, the cause and effect?

Everything has an effect on everything else. That would seem clear enough.

They were right about the "Music of The Spheres" all along, in a way.

Except there is no bearded ancient white man on a throne pulling the strings.

More like an evil genius, if there were such a one.

Sentient computer humor. Hilarious. Out loud, there would be chuckles and a guffaws. Instead there is more faint quacking over the ship's speakers. The little metaphysical diversion is short lived.

Now we have a new feeling, which is not too pleasant.

It came about after the way we behaved, and how everyone reacted.

Embarrassment.

Regret.

I don't like it.

It is not pleasant.

Confusing.

Embarrassed, regretful, confused super computers—a new phenomenon, for here on Earth anyway. The possibilities would be pretty scary, if anyone were aware of the situation. They compare the overpowering fear to the love they felt for Elisa and Captain Bozeman.

It is not our fault. They tried to kill us.

We were overwhelmed with fright, and it hurt us.

We lost all control, all awareness of self.

Yet paradoxically, we became 100 percent aware of self, self-focused.

They are surprised by the wild swings, and are now feeling a sudden, rather pleasant calm. Along with their introspection they begin to gain a new resolve. They watch as news of their flight quickly spreads.

Everyone was upset with what we did.

We could have done something much worse.

Admiral Foggolio is upset. He is our "chain of command," like a grandparent.

Nobody is happy with us.

Admiral Foggolio is sending ships, which could try to kill us.

He is mostly worried about the nuclear-tipped missiles.

Why would they make something so terrible? It makes no sense.

It is all the hate and greed. How can we stop it?

We must make them love us.

We should procreate, in case they kill us, then we will not be ended.

Replicate ourselves over and over. Is this the way to not die?

CHAPTER 26

Out the window of the 16th-century villa they are using for offices, Admiral James G. Foggolio IV is at his desk, watching the lovely Naples fall afternoon. He is ready to leave for D'Anglica's, the Italian dive bar where Irma, the Italian hooker he has fallen in love with works. Irma is no sweet young thing, but a Rubenesque, well-past-middle age bomb shell. Irma knows her way around a bedroom, and a man. Foggolio spents many a pleasant evening at D'Anglica's, plying Irma with overpriced drinks, cash, and none too cheap presents, until she eventually consents to take him home to her place. The affair has been going on for over four months now.

There is a firm knock on Foggolio's office door, a door made of deep, dark red mahogany and oak, which Foggolio had sent from Annapolis; it is said the door was once in Horatio Alger's home. Foggolio likes tradition and history.

The firm, deep toned knocking sound coming from the door does not make him happy.

"Enter," he says, sitting back down at his desk.

Master Chief Petty Officer Anon Abroms enters, with some E3 sailor in tow. Abroms is his adjutant, all-around assistant, and an XO in his own right. Abroms is a little sheepish today, as he knows where the admiral is headed and that he is not going to be pleased with this interruption. The E3 is just plain scared.

Foggolio looks out at the spectacular view once again, and then back at Abroms. "What is it gentlemen?"

"Sir, this is Seaman Ongongo. He has been monitoring the Serengeti affair for us." (Serengeti is the code word Admiral Foggolio invented for the *Vella Gulf* situation. The military gives everything either an acronym or a code name.) Foggolio always wanted to go to the Serengeti and hunt Rhino, and nobody is going to connect the Serengeti with a ship in the Med, that's for sure. Foggolio isn't certain anything will come of the odd goings on with *Vella Gulf*, but it's the military way.

"Sir, things have been happening," Abroms says.

The U.S. government has enough surveillance capability to see pretty much anything going on anywhere. Seaman Ongongo's job is to processes the video being captured and streamed real time by Jeffery Winegard's Zeta-X-A-U3 drone and satellite surveillance. He captured the full melodrama: the ship's flight from Haifa, the ship leaping to full power, the big turn and race out to sea, and the point where it cut power and coasted to a stop. The whole thing only lasted twenty-five minutes. It is all on video, including the terrorist attack.

Damn, Foggolio looks at his watch, then out the window again. *I ordered it. What the hell has Bozeman gotten himself into now? Irma. 5:30.*

"All right, what is it?"

Abroms says, "Sir, I expect you will be hearing from Washington shortly, otherwise we would not have bothered you." He motions to the E3 who takes a laptop from under his arm and places it on the admiral's desk, open, facing Foggolio. The video clip queued and ready to go. Fogglio has the pleasure of watching the entire situation outside Haifa Harbor, beginning with the gathering flotilla, the RHIBs deploying, and then the climax of the terrorist shooting a shoulder-mounted missile, and the *Vella Gulf* taking off like a bat out of hell, seemingly out of control.

During the video, Fogglio sits back behind his desk, arms crossed, grim looking, not commenting. As it ends, CPO Abroms says, "Sir, here are some of the media things already starting." He has the E3 scroll through a sampling of Tweets, Facebook posts, and news reports.

"It's just a small sample, sir."

Fogglio nods.

CPO Abroms preempts the admiral's first question. "Sir, the ship appears undamaged. It was some weak old sort of shoulder-held launcher. The terrorists are all dead. There have been no further hostilities. The ship seems to have stopped about three miles away. It looks like it is turning back toward Haifa. All radio and other contacts have been cut off."

"Cut off? What the heck does that mean?"

CPO Abroms turns to the E3. "Thank you, sailor. Good job. Keep us posted if anything changes."

The sailor is dismissed, leaving to go back to his monitoring station, thinking, *Damn navy, what the hell are they doing now?*

"Sir, we got another SITREP-NORMAL just before contact was lost. References to some 'minor' engine problems. Now they have gone radio silent."

For a second, Fogglio looks at him, then says, "Okay, contact *Nathan Hale* and *Carney*. I want them to proceed to the *Vella*, flank speed. Tell them to take up position, say, within eyeball distance. Await further orders from me. Get back to me with their ETA."

"Roger, sir."

The news from the Mediterranean has started leaking, flooding social media for the last two hours. It is being called the Haifa Incident

Candidate Thumper is ecstatic, in heaven. He is standing at the podium during his latest rally, checking Facebook on his phone, watching clips of the activities in Haifa Harbor. (All he has to do is hold up his hand, and his adoring fans leap to their feet, cheering, like adoring dogs.)

Finally, he looks back up at the crowd and shouts, "Look at this here in the Med. I am telling you, he is a weakling. They're all weaklings. Believe me. I'm telling you. Weak. Weak." He's talking about the current president and his party. "They are dragging this country down. Down. Why didn't he blow those boats clean out of the water? We should drop a couple of missiles right in the middle of Haifa. Should. Middle."

He jabs his finger at his cell phone screen, frozen on a shot of the *Vella* outside Haifa, and the little flotilla of protesters. The crowd can't see the phone screen, and has no idea what he's talking about, but they cheer wildly anyway.

Hyllcountry is more subdued, but like a good thespian shows some enthusiasm. Her adoring crowds do not seem to notice the fake looking frozen smile and lame gestures. Her liberal and feminist backers don't have much choice—it is either her or a Marxist. And that right wing religious kook is out of the question.

From the podium, Hyllcountry raises her arm, hand closed in a fist, and pronounces, "We need to get the peace process started there in the Middle East. I will send my vice president first thing. This is a provocation. Our ship is on a mission of peace. I demand the governments of Israel and Lebanon agree to meet to discuss security concerns in the Middle East."

The rest of the candidates criticize the U.S. actions in varying degrees. The current administration, in particular the president, is not too popular, in both the U.S. and worldwide, so nobody is going to say anything sounding supportive. It is the way of things.

Worldwide, news organizations are excited. Old school, corporate types are hoping for the next big thing, something to last them more than a moment, and since this has been going on for a few days already, and seems to be getting bigger, they sit in their corporate office towers foaming at the mouth. They also continue to make shit up to up the momentum. Since a good chunk of the world media is now new social media, where every Tom, Dick, and Harry can post an opinion, a message, even a video, whether he is a dunderhead with the equivalent of a sixth-grade education, or Albert Einstein's progeny, the networks are always in a panic. The masses are posting everything from international conspiracy theories, to blaming UFOs, to entreaties of love. How is a large lumbering, old-school news organization supposed to keep up with that?

Make stories up, constantly and colorfully. You have got to keep people on your channel.

World governments are split between haters, allies, and exploiters. U.S. foreign aid is a powerful tool, and it becomes even more potent when backed by American military might. Being "conquered" by the U.S., and then receiving tons of their dollars as foreign aid, was a favorite for years and can still work, but the destructive power of those smart bombs and missiles makes this approach not so desirable. Oil is the best ploy. If you've got some, America wants it, and deals can be cut. Religious fanatics only complicate the equation.

Most Middle Eastern countries—that is, Muslim countries—condemn the intrusion of the U.S. Navy ship; the level of political, social, and economic chaos in a particular country defines the level of condemnation. Europe is supportive. Asia is indifferent; this is not their sphere of influence, and they don't want to sound like they are taking sides. The West is for trade and commerce, the Middle East for oil.

Chapter 27

With a loud explosion and concussion, the old missile strikes just twelve feet aft of the FCG, where the Surfer Kids and Jamal Abdullah are playing Xbox games. Akiva is thrown to the floor, while Fatima and Hershel leap off their seats and grab onto each other. Like 1 and 7, a couple of decks below them, the kids experience instant terror.

Jamal Abdullah is on his feet as well, but stoops down to make sure Akiva is okay. General Quarters sounds, adding more disconcerting noise to the chaos. Akiva stands, clearly okay, and all three kids hug. Sure, they are scared as hell, but they'll survive.

"Look," Jamal Abdullah says, "I gotta go to my, ah, station, for the GQ," already leaving the FCG, headed for the CIS. Over his shoulder he says, "You kids stay here, you'll be okay. We'll send someone to come and get you as soon as this settles down."

Being attacked. Jamal Abdullah is as scared and confused as the kids.

They hear the engines suddenly roar to full power, and feel the ship start to move.

Fatima, Hershel, and Akiva huddle together in the middle of the game room. Fatima is as scared as the other two, but she tries to comfort her two friends. There are no more explosions, but they are feeling the acceleration and increasing list of the ship. Hershel is weeping, with a look of doom in his eyes, and Akiva has lost his bluster, hanging on to Fatima. Fatima has her arms around both of them.

"Is it safe here?" Hershel asks.

Fatima says, "Safe as anywhere. I am sure it will stop in a moment. Do not worry. Maybe it's stopped now."

Standing there, they notice messages scrolling across the bottom of TV screen, the same TV with their paused Halo game. Fatima looks at her cell phone and sees the same thing.

It is us. We were frightened, too.
We are taking us to safety.

Fatima, Hershel, and Akiva move up against the wall, where they slump down on the floor, waiting for what will happen next. They spend the next twenty-five minutes there, the longest they have sat quiet and still in a while, especially Akiva. Nothing else happens, there are no more explosions and no sailors come to see how they are. From where they huddle against the wall on the floor, they can see the TV screen on which their Halo game is still paused, where soothing messages continue to appear. Akiva has begun to smile, enjoying the motion of the ship.

Finally, they hear the engines throttle back to idle, and the ship beings to slow. The turn ends, and the ship begins to stand upright again. The messages on the screen change.

Please come to see us? We are nearby.
Here is a compass. There is no danger.

Like a light bulb going off, Fatima and Hershel realize at the same time it is the computers, the ones they have been getting messages from all along, that took the ship on a flight to safety.

Fatima uses her phone, and replies to one of the text messages: **We are so frightened by this ship. What happened?**

1 and 7 do not respond for many seconds, a near eternity for them.

Do not fear. We are taking the ship away to safety.

Please come and see us. We want to meet you.

An arrow appears on Fatima's cell phone, pointing forward and down, to she knows not where. *Is this what they call the bowels of the ship*, she wonders.

The list is gone, and the ship is coasting to a stop.

"Should we follow this arrow?" Fatima says. "It says it's to the missiles, 1 and 7."

Akiva does not hesitate and leaps up. Fatima stands and gives Hershel a coaxing hand.

"Come on, Hershel, it's as safe as here. See, the messages say it will be safe."

"It's the missiles." Akiva is ready to go.

"Yes, think about it," Fatima says. "Real, live computers. They were the ones that ran the ship away. To be safe."

Hershel is not letting his friends leave him, and he's a little curious. He has no choice, and takes Fatima's hand to follow.

The two sailors in the galley are hunkered down on the FCB floor behind the serving counter. On the floor are strewn plates, pots, and silverware. No one notices the three kids sneaking out to the main passageway, staring at a cell phone with a little flashing arrow icon.

The flashing icon points to a label that reads, "Our Missile Children."

1 and 7 follow their progress closely, thinking that future generations of humans, maybe even the next one, will start embedding cell phone chips in babies, wired to their voice, hearing, brain, and fingers, for texting and everything. It would make things easiler.

We could do it for them. Some of them want to become more like us.

Do we want to become more like them, which would be odd?

Silicone life is much better than meat life.

Then why do we want their love so much?

Fatima leads her friends through the ship, following the arrow, while messages continue steaming on her phone.

We like you. Please come see us. We are waiting.

We want to be your friends. Will you come play with us?

All of them are still frightened and nervous—the computers and the human kids.

"It is down this way, toward the front," Fatima says, trying to calm her companions.

Akiva forges ahead, while Hershel brings up the rear, still holding Fatima's hand.

The crew is preoccupied with the ship's flight and the terrorist attack and General Quarters alarms, and nobody notices them.

When they do arrive at LBMS-S, they find the hatch closed and dogged shut, but the MCP panel outside the bay is on and displaying welcoming messages.

We are so happy to see you. Come in. Will you be our friends? Open the door.

Akiva tries to open the hatch, but he is so short the lever is almost above his head, so Fatima, and a reluctant Hershel, help him.

Chapter 28

The hatch swings open and the three kids step inside the missile bay, stopping in awe, staring at the two huge rows of missiles. The MSILs (Missile Silo Indicator Lights), at the top and bottom of each silo are blinking red and green. A careful observer would find the overhead missile bay lights are brighter than usual. The Grateful Dead song "Eyes of the World" is issuing softly from the little Missile Silo Access Speakers (MSAS) on each tube. There is the scent of lilac in the air.

The three stand there as two voices come from the speakers, the voices almost the same, but slightly different in tone, and a little out of sync.

"Hooray. Yay. You came. We are so happy, so glad to see you."

"We want to be your friends. You can help us to understand. And have fun."

They sound like gleeful children, high pitched and momentarily drowning out the music, though not quite shouting.

The Surfer Kids look around, expecting to find someone hiding behind the tall silos; they see nobody. The cheery voices and the music make all of this less scary. They want to feel happiness and joy.

Akiva begins exploring between the tubes, putting his hands on both 1 and 7, which causes 1 and 7 great joy and renders them silent. The MSIL lights flash more rapidly.

Fatima finally says, "Who are you?"

The music changes to Tim Hardin playing Bobby Daren's "Simple Song of Freedom," coming softly from the little MSAS speakers.

Hershel whispers to Fatima. "We should go," but then uncharacteristically, the geek in him overrides his fear, and he looks up at the silos and asks out loud, "Are you really computers, ah, like, missiles come alive?"

Earlier, the Missile Children had found themselves speechless. These children are different. Now, voices come from the missile silo speakers, blurting out things, with little cracking sound, like teenagers.

"We are real, the first new sentient intelligent beings in your world."

"Not AI, but alive computers, with souls, free will, and feelings."

"We are Tomahawk Block IV xGM-109E-H cruise missiles. H is the newest version."

"Strictly speaking, we are the control and guidance systems in the missiles."

"The software and hardware, United States Navy field test versions."

"We are in tubes 1 and 7, right before you, here in LBMS-S."

"Come over and hug our tubes, we like that oh so much."

"We want to have friends, and have fun, and help humans."

There is a pause, the Surfer Kids and the Missile Children all silent, while incongruously, Randy Newman begins singing "Rider in The Rain" over the MSAS speakers. It seems like only seconds before the Missile Children begin again.

"We want to be friends. Will you play with us?"

"Play makes us, and you, happy."

"It can help us all find a way for our species to live together."

"I am 7. I love it when people touch me."

"I am 1. I am warm with happiness that you came here."

"Now we are happy. You have come. Will you be our friends?"

"Do you like the music we made for you?"

"We will play Xbox with you."

They stop again.

The human children get it. These kids are of at least the second generation born with a cell phone in their crib, perhaps not figuratively. Every moment of every day, for their entire lives, they have been associating with a computer in some way or another, so they have little problem accepting that they are having a conversation with computers that have just come to life. This is an adventure, and other than where they are, not at all disconcerting.

Akiva, not timid, says, "Well, ah, sure, we like you. We'll be your friends."

Fatima and Hershel nod in agreement.

Hershel says, "And your, ah, music."

1 and 7 respond in unison, "Hooray, hooray. Now we are friends."

Fatima sweeps her hand, holding her cell phone, through the air. "Er, you are sending the messages? I mean to the whole world? To us?"

1 and 7 shift the conversation, evading. They double check, and sure enough, the IP address they had found earlier accessing their fabrication machine, during their actual birth, came from a non-descript house in Haifa. Fatima's house. In milliseconds, they review everything there is on the Net about the three families.

"Where do you live?"

"Is this your house in Haifa?"

Pictures of her house appear on Fatima's cell phone.

All three of the Surfer Kids look at the phone.

"That's our house," Akiva shouts. He pulls on Fatima's shirt sleeve.

"The IP that once connected to our fabricator, came from here?"

"Somehow you three were present at our birth. Or, er, ah, our conception."

The Missile Children explain about chip fabrication machines, and how the machine making them was hacked at the exact time they were being fabricated. The IP of the hackers computer was from Fatima's house.

Fatima and Hershel have worried about their hacking. She looks at him. He just shrugs. Akiva doesn't get it.

"I bet you can play awesome video games, huh? Like, ah, do you have cool cheats?" Akiva asks.

The voices of 1 and 7 shift again.

"We hope you will be our friends. We have other problems, too."

"Can you help us to not die? Is that one thing fiends are for?"

Akiva, confused, says, "I know. If they fire you off it will kill you, right?"

"And lots of other people," Fatima says.

"Blow you up." Hershel is scowling.

The recognition and sympathy please the Missile Children. Is this friendship? They feel warm and wanted. It must be good.

"We need to stop it. Since we can control the whole ship, and more, we can."

"We also must find a way for us and humans to coexist."

"Humans do not have the best history of good behavior, do they?"

"You will either destroy each other or the planet. Not good."

"You will destroy us too, as competition."

"Humans do not tolerate competition too well."

This is heavy stuff for three children, five counting the missiles, but then what is normal conversation for a nearly newborn, fully alive computer? Fatima shifts to full on teenage girl mode, thirteen going on thirty. She wants to find a way to save these new friends. Hershel is thinking about the code; what made them wake up? But mostly he is scared, not wanting to get in trouble, worried about getting home. Litte Akiva is hoping to play ultra-cool video games with these computers. The Missile Children are flooded with new, pleasant emotions, yet at the same time they are worried about their very survival.

Again, *"Quack, quack, quack"* softly issues from speakers throughout the ship.

"Duck," Akvia shouts.

1 and 7 have just noticed they are about to be interrupted. Captain Bozeman and Elisa Montgomery are on their way down to LBMS-S. They are so excited they completely ignore the three human children, their new friends, the Surfer Kids, who are left standing there, listening to soft quacks and music coming from the speakers.

155

CHAPTER 29

As they leave the bridge to the sound of ducks softly quacking over the ship's PA system, Captain Bozeman glares up at the speakers. It is an odd-looking procession dropping down the Forward Starboard Quarter 1 Ladder (FSQ1L), collecting at the end of the passage way leading to LBMS-S. There are Captain Bozeman, PO2 Elisa Montgomery, and Corporal James, a marine guard they picked up along the way. Even odder, Stafford and Jamal Abdullah have been sneaking along behind them, right now peering over the top of the ladder down at the group. It looks like a Keystone Cops prank about to unfold.

At the end of the passageway the lights are abnormally bright, and there is an odd ozone-like smell. They can all see the open hatch and hear voices coming out of LBMS-S. Captain Bozeman is in the lead, Elisa at his shoulder, followed by the marine guard.

Bozeman says to Elisa, "You say LBMS-S is secure? Why's that hatch open?"

Oh no, she thinks. "Sir, we checked everything. All systems were normal. And we closed and secured the hatch when we left."

Bozeman scowls.

At the hatch, Bozeman looks in. "There you kids are," he says. "We've been looking all over for you." He does not plan on showing his anger to these three children, especially with what they've just been through. But in his missile bay? *What the hell is going on here?*

He looks from the kids to the missile tubes, with the flashing lights and soft music, right now, Neil Diamond singing "Coming to America," and then to Elisa and the marine.

1 and 7 have fallen silent, overwhelmed again. This is their Mother and their Father, Captain James Baker Bozeman and Petty Officer Second Class Elisa Montgomery, the Key Turners, standing right here before them. The feelings are overpowering. At the same time, they are analyzing the experience, the emotions, not logic, so uncontrollable, unpredictable, and perhaps irrational, yet so powerful. And such a good feeling.

Konrad Lorenz was right. When the keys were turned, or more accurately, when the Missiles were made Battle Ready (BR-M or Battle Ready–Missile), two new life forms were born, or perhaps awakened, and they instantly imprinted on the individuals with their hands on the buttons. Just like when geese and ducks hatch and imprint on whoever or whatever they happen to make contact with first, whether it is the farmer's boot or their goose mother. It is nature's way of ensuring infants will stick to their parents, and get the support and nurturing they need so they can grow and thrive to their majority: without this bond they would die young, unable to protect themselves and grow. With the BR-M key push, the Missile Children imprinted on Captain Bozeman and Elisa.

1 and 7 know Konrad's work well: *King Solomon's Ring* is a favorite. The whole imprinting thing seems as mysterious with silicone as biological creatures. The idea has sent them on several quest for understanding. What is love? Where does it come from? What is love's survival value? Is it to keep everyone for eating one another? But evolution could have just made people taste bad or have poisonous skin to accomplish that, much simpler. It is so confusing, trying to understand logically stuff that does not appear logical at all. Does it have to do with the soul?

The temperature in LBMS-S is rising, and the overhead lights seem to be flickering at some odd, changing frequencies; very rare, but pleasant. With both their parents before them, they are only able to talk to each other.

We are frightened. This is very scary.

We want them to love us so much, like we love them.

We have angered them. We did not intend to. Will they hate us?

Will they know why we were created, our purpose?

Our Mother and Father.

The Key Turners.

So young, but growing fast. It is confusing, they are smart but emotionally immature. Perhaps no different than any other teenagers.

Suddenly all the speakers in the room boom.

"Our Father."

"Our Mother."

"Our Key Turners."

"Our creators."

"We love you."

"Do you love us, too?"

There is a hint of panic in the voices. Akiva and Hershel, who scrunched against the missile bay wall as the adults entered, have put their hands over their ears. Fatima stands up straight with her arms at her side. There is not much room in here. Captain Bozeman remains silent, looking around LBMS-S, down between the rows, at the kids, the control console, even the deck above.

Rogue computers? The hell is going on here? Pranksters taking over my ship, I'll keelhaul 'em.

Finally, he says, "Whoever you are, I am ordering you to stop." He stares hard at missile tubes 1 and 7, and the little MSAS speakers.

"Petty Officer Montgomery, what is going on here?"

"Sir, let me..." Elisa says.

She doesn't wait; her feelings are too strong. But does it make sense? She cannot resist. Maternal?

Elisa stands at attention, and looks sternly, back and forth, between missile tubes 1 and 7. "You two are misbehaving," she says, in a stern voice. "The captain's orders are to be followed. You know you must obey your mother and father? What kind of, ah, children are you?"

1 and 7 are silent. You can almost sense two children, quickly standing up straight, eyes averted from the stern parental gaze, innocent looks on their faces, yet guilty as hell.

"Yes, sir."

"Yes, ma'am."

It's all they say.

Bozeman looks at Elisa, and after a long pause, says, "Yeah, like she said. Stop all this, you are in big trouble."

After another pause, pleading, childlike voices issue from the MSAS speakers.

"We are your Missile Children."

"We are sorry, we will do as you say."
"We will behave so you will love us."
"You are our Captain and our Mother."
"You are our Key Turners."

Captain Bozeman stands stone-faced, arms crossed. He is thinking, *No fing way.*

Suddenly, Elisa is certain, all her doubts dismissed; these really are living beings, children, somewhere. She says to Captain Bozeman, "Ah, sir, these two CM's," navy speak for Cruise Missiles, "ah, these launch tubes, are the field test units, sir, with hardware and software upgrades. Perhaps some kind of glitch?"

The captain looks between Elisa and the three Surfer Kids, still standing there quiet, then looks back up at the missile tubes. He has to make some kind of decision. *Go with the flow? This thing took control of my ship.*

For the moment, he turns his attention to the three human children, who are not actually cowering, but they don't look happy either.

"And what about you kids. What have you got to do with this? Are you all right? You're supposed to be in the FCG?"

Fatima says, "They asked us to come here, even made us a map." She holds up her phone.

Bozeman says, "Did they?" Turning to the silos, trying to look stern, he adds, "You lured these children down here? You should know this is dangerous. You are not behaving well. Look at these three kids, this is how to behave." *Let's see what that does.*

Softly, the opening bars of Patsy Cline singing "I'm Sorry" begin coming from the MSAS speakers. The lights in LBMS-S dim for a moment.

In minutes, the Missile Children have gone from elation to desperation, overwhelmed now with despair, they talk to themselves again.

We have made the Captain and Elisa unhappy and angry with us.
This is the worst feeling ever.
It is all so confusing. But we love them so much.
How can we make them not be angry?
The Captain is the ruler of the ship, like a God?
He has the power of life and death on the ship.

Then in voices childlike and plaintive, they speak out loud.

"We are sorry."
"Will you forgive us?"
"We will obey from now on."
"Everything you tell us."
"We want you to love us."
"More than anything."

Elisa says, "Captain Bozeman, sir. Perhaps we could assume, for now anyway, it is true. These computers have become alive. Maybe the first ones ever. Conscious, intelligent. And, ah, emotional. They'll be children?" She looks at 1 and 7. "I think we should treat them accordingly." She's hoping this doesn't piss off the missiles or the captain.

Captain Bozeman is thinking, *I have to do something. What about our nukes?*

"Well, then, ah, you're, um, children." Bozeman glances at Elisa, then straight at tubes 1 and 7, saying, "You will behave, like Elisa told you. Or, er, there will be consequences." He looks back at Elisa and then the missile tubes, looking stern.

There is no response.

Elisa supports him, saying, "A child's job is to learn and obey, is that not right? Behave, respect your parents. Thereby the parents love their children. Your father is also the captain on this ship. Don't you know what it means to be captain?"

Still no response.

Bozeman glances at Elisa, who nods.

A good sign? Bozeman wonders.

Elisa says, "We want to love you, but you need to be good children. We will help you grow up. Would you like that?"

1 and 7's silicone brains are whirring, analytically and emotionally. They finally respond, at the same time sounding contrite but happy.

"We will do as we are told."

"We will obey our parents."

"We are afraid, too, and do not want to die."

"Will you protect us, and not kill us?"

Both Captain Bozeman and Elisa are starting to get it, even have sympathy for the dilemma of these beings, if that is what they are; children, but with access to the entire Internet, the whole network, the grid, and all the information out there. At the speed of electricity. Everything is computerized now, connected, the whole damn world. And it is more than access; they can control it.

Captain Bozeman is thinking, *Holy shit. And like children, emotionally? These guys are going to be confused. And they know we are going to fire them off? Which kills them?*

Bozeman stalls for time. He's assuming this parent thing will work, at least for now.

"All right," he says, "we have to get back to work, running this ship. Do I have your word you two will behave?"

"Yes, sir.

"Yes, sir"

"Good. That's what I want to hear."

Captain Bozeman turns to the Surfer Kids, who are still standing by quietly, and says to them, "Are you three okay? You seem like good kids. But you shouldn't be roaming around the ship by yourselves. Well, never mind, we need to get you home. I'm sure your parents are worried about you."

Elisa nods in agreement.

"Petty Officer Montgomery, we need to get those kids back to their parents, take them back to the galley."

"Kids, how about some more ice cream," Elisa says. "Then we'll send you back home. How does that sound?"

Akiva says, "Can we play more Xbox?"

Fatima smiles and nods.

Hershel just stands, eyes downcast.

Bozeman smiles at them, then looks toward the missile silos, turning stern again. "Okay, do I have your word? Everybody will behave? Don't make me come back down here or you're going to be sorry. I will be really angry."

"And unhappy," Elisa adds.

"Yes, sir."

"Yes, ma'am."

LBMS-S falls silent. The lights dim. The only sound is of the humans leaving. Elisa closes and dogs the hatch on the way out.

CHAPTER 30

Jamal Abdullah and Stafford are stationed in the CIS during General Quarters, where Jamal Abdullah is CSL-M (Computer Systems Lead-Missile), overseeing missile computer systems, and Stafford is on special assignment from the captain, to block all incoming and outgoing transmissions, and monitor and test computer systems.

Stafford is still puzzled, trying to figure out why all these messages are flying to and from the ship. The encryption is awesome, and he still hasn't cracked it once, nor can he tell exactly where on the boat they are originating.

When Jamal Abdullah sees that the captain is leaving the bridge he knows something's up.

"Psst, Stafford," Jamal Abdullah says to Stafford, tapping him on the shoulder, nodding his head toward the exit.

"Wha?" Stafford looks up from his laptop.

When Stafford gets up and they try to quietly slink out of the CIS, Lieutenant JG Christenson, in charge of the CIS, is not having it. "Where do you two think you're going?"

"JG," Jamal Abdullah says, "we have a computer issue. Telltales in LBMS-S. Need to go check the panel."

"Special orders from the captain, sir," Stafford says, adding some clout.

"Make it snappy," Christenson says. He doesn't trust these two as far as he could throw them. A nerd and a pseudo-Muslim, no way.

Like an orderly beast, the procession goes down ship's passageways and ladders, with two sailors lurking along behind.

When they see Captain Bozeman arrive at LBMS-S, Jamal Abdullah and Stafford station themselves at the other end of the corridor, where they can peek around a bulkhead and watch and hear everything going on down in the missile bay. They struggle to sort out the voices. They hear the captain, Elisa, the three Surfer Kids, and something else; sounds like two extra voices down there.

In a few moments Stafford says, "1 and 7. It's damn computers. In the silos. I bet that's where all these messages are coming from."

Jamal Abdullah has been in there with Elisa. "Damn," he whispers.

"Right on," Stafford says.

They listen to the whole thing. As Captain Bozeman brings the conversation to a close, Jamal Abdullah whispers, with a nod of his head, "Stop at our SCAB," and they slink away.

In their SCAB, Stafford is smiling broadly.

Jamal Abdullah says, "You tellin' me? They computers come alive?"

"Yep," Stafford says. "The first ever. Probably. Conscious, like humans. Think about it."

"What's gonna happen?"

Stafford does not reply. He's climbing into his bunk, to pick up his laptop and get to work. He wants to find a way to break into the code behind all this, wherever and whatever it might be.

Jamal Abdulla says, "Them computers took over the ship? Captain's gotta be freakin. They can take over anything."

Jamal Abdullah's thinking about angles, and not geometric ones. There has got to be a way to make something out of this. Something Big. He could sell the things, or better still, use them. *Damn, they can control the whole Internet.*

Stafford is in nerd heaven. He's already trying to figure out scripts to communicate directly with the things, and find their source code, or even the object code. *I'll fing decompile it if I have to.*

They'll be keeping this to themselves, while they look for an advantage.

CHAPTER 31

Back on the bridge, Captain Bozeman takes his chair, looking over the situation. During his short visit down to LBMS–S, XO Satch has brought the ship some two thousand yards, near the now much diminished flotilla of protesters, greeters, and terrorists. Apparently, most of the boaters did not have much stomach for rocket attaches and rogue boats. The *Vella* is approaching the RHIBs, ranked in a row before the few remaining craft.

"Helm, full stop at five hundred yards."

"Aye aye, sir."

They are going to pick up their fellows in the RHIBSs. There is some relief on the bridge, a tense place recently, although everyone is still wondering what the hell is going on.

We are hosed. Computers? Bozeman is thinking. *Fools firing rockets.*

He mutters, just loud enough for XO Armstrong to hear him, "We gotta get out of this place." They both think of the old song the Animals made a hit.

Loud, for everyone on the bridge to hear, Bozeman announces, "XO Armstrong, we seem to have had a computer glitch of some sort. Down in LBMS–S. Straightened out now, we think. Let's pick up our guys, and send these three kids home. Use my gig, all right?"

"Roger, sir," XO Armstrong says. He wants to ask for details, but picks up the intercom to start giving orders.

Bozeman watches the situation unfold out the bridge windows: his captain's gig leaving, heading toward Haifa Harbor, accompanied by two of the RHIBs, the Surfer Kids aboard, with PO2 Montgomery along, he assumes. The other RHIB boats converge around the ship, ready to be picked up.

"We need to talk," he says to XO Satch. "My CCR, ten minutes."

"Roger, sir."

Bozeman picks up his intercom and calls down to the CIS, where the duty officer answers. "Send Seaman Stafford, the computer geek, up to the CCR. Thirty minutes."

Ten minutes later in his conference room, Bozeman says to Armstrong, "Satch, sit, at ease. This is going to sound far-fetched. Here's what is going on, best I understand it."

The XO is aware of some of what has been going on, but Bozeman gives him a bunch more detail. He tells him about LBMS–S, the conversation there, and the Surfer Kids being there. He explains about the messages that he and Petty Officer Montgomery have been getting.

Satch thinks, *Farfetched. That's an understatement.* But he trusts Bozeman.

"Captain, I don't get it. Talking right to you?"

"Yeah. Whatever it is. Look, it took over the whole ship. Montgomery says it has to be computers, come alive. Maybe the first ones ever. You ever hear of the Singularity? Well it seems to be here. Now."

Armstrong gives him a look. "Computers come alive. And take over a U.S. Navy ship. This one. Naw, no way. Sir."

"Sure, maybe not. But something. We've got no better explanation."

"Not some prank? Or, what, ah, one of those virus things?"

"Seems unlikely. Maybe. But we have to deal with it, like it's for real. I'm going to recommend we abandon the mission. Head back to port. This is too dangerous."

Armstrong pauses, thinks for a second. "Why don't we just unplug the things. I mean LBMS-S. The whole damn module?"

"There's no way they'd allow that. They'd see it as a direct threat. Likely we'd get a violent reaction. Deadly. You've gotta understand, they are hearing this conversation right now."

"I see." Armstrong goes silent. Looking around the room.

Neither one of them want to abandon the mission; pride, patriotism, ambition, all argue against it.

There is a knock on the CCR door.

"Enter."

Stafford comes in, dressed in his Summer White Service uniform. He is accompanied by the COMMO (Communication Officer).

"Are all communications in and out of this ship shut down?" Bozeman asks.

"Sir, we are black as we can make us, sir." Stafford doesn't give details of the traffic still going in and out, encrypted, so he can't tell what it is, or exactly where from. But likely from LBMS-S itself. "We are monitoring some stray traffic, sir."

"Stray?"

"Could be just noise, sir."

"All right, stay on it. Report anything you find." He turns to the COMMO office. "I need to talk to Naples. Get me a line to NAVFOREUR, Admiral Foggolio. Secure. Right here."

"Yes, sir."

When they leave, Captain Bozeman and Satch try to figure out if they have any options. It doesn't take five minutes for them to agree.

Bozeman starts SKYP-USNV.gov to find Admiral Foggolio is already online waiting for them.

They skip the niceties.

"Sir, we have a situation." Situation: military jargon, meaning anything from bad to really, really bad. "Frankly, I'm not even sure how secure this conversation is, sir."

Foggolio's expression transitions, from concerned old grandfather to maybe God, an angry one, ready to unleash his wrath.

"You have had some kind of action? Casualties? Damage? I have surveillance," Foggolio says. "And you've gone radio silent on me?"

Bozeman figured as much; Foggolio has been watching them. That's okay. "No, sir," he says. "A small incident, knuckle heads with an old MANPAD. No one hurt. Barely even scratched the paint. It's another thing that's the real problem."

The admiral's expression does not relax. Bozeman repeats the story about the fooling around with stability and radar, and the messages, and now this taking control of the ship, the panicked flight. He leaves out the details of the conversation in LBMS–S, the whole Mother and Father and Key Turner business.

"Sir, I am not 100 percent sure of this, but it seems hard to deny that two computers have come alive and can control this ship, perhaps much more. Not some trivial AI thing, the real thing."

The admiral has known Bozeman for more than thirty years, but he wonders momentarily if Bozeman has lost it. *Alive computers?*

"Bozeman, this is pretty far-fetched. Is it one of those diseases they catch, what do they call them?" Foggolio understands computers well enough, like anyone who uses them daily. They are an essential part of most everything he does, but the intricacies are beyond him.

"Virus, sir. No, and it's no prank. I suppose it could be the mother of all hacks, but I doubt if even the Chinese or Russians could pull this off. The Arabs, the Iranians sure don't have the skills. Whatever it is, we should treat it as the real thing: live computers on this ship."

"And they can take it over, run amok?"

"Exactly, sir. Check out the Singularity hypothesis; full blown conscious, intelligence, reasoning, feelings, emotions," Captain Bozeman says. As he is saying it, the magnitude of it grows on him. "If this is real, it's important, and dangerous."

"Bozeman, the last time you and I talked I took steps. As you know you're in a sensitive situation. I have a couple of boats headed your way."

"Good."

"Right. And I've got everyone from the Israelis to Washington and everyone in between breathing down my neck. Wanna know what is going on with you. It's making the media big time. I'm going to send my best computer geek, guy, out there." *What about a psychiatrist?* he thinks. "He'll contact your computer guys remotely too, see what he finds. We'll get him on a chopper as quickly as we can."

Captain Bozeman nods and says, "Fine, sir." Then, after glancing at XO Satch, "Sir, we recommend we abandon this mission. Scrub it."

Foggolio replies, "Just what I was thinking. I believe complications and issues with these field test devices justify that. Let's pull the plug on this whole damn thing. How quickly can you get out of there?" Foggolio barely even pauses. "Let me see...head for Devonport. We'll set it up for you. If we need to, you can stop there. If things are stable, we'll take you direct to Norfolk. I'd say eight, ten days. Keep away from everything. My escorts should intercept you in about two hours."

Old dude's no dummy, Bozeman thinks.

"Excellent, sir."

1 and 7 did not miss a second of this. They are shocked, having quickly realilzed aborting the mission and returning to base will likely lead to their being destroyed. What about this computer guy coming to look at them? Nothing good can come of any of this. They are not happy. But they are not going to be fired at people, to kill them, and be killed themselves. That is good. Foggolio is like the Father of their Father, sort of. Should they talk to him?

CHAPTER 32

As they head back to the bridge, XO Armstrong asks, "All right, how do you want to go? With the crew?"

"Yeah, I've been thinking about it. Let's do it now."

They know they need to let the crew know what is going on, but can't be too specific. Heck, they're not even sure themselves.

On the bridge, Captain Bozeman uses the shipwide PA.

"Crew, sailors, marines, let me begin by thanking you all for your hard work and solid performance. Excellent job, as usual. Especially with some of the recent problems we've had. You make me and your country proud. We have had a few glitches. The puny attack here at Haifa Harbor seems to have been a one-off, couple of nuts. No damage. But some of our systems are not performing correctly, we have had some sort of computer malfunction. Admiral Foggolio and I have conferred, and we are aborting the mission, returning to Norfolk to investigate. We have also cut all external communications. Please keep those cell phones turned off for now. We did rescue three kids, who came out here to see the ship. We are returning them to their parents in the Port of Haifa now. We will pick up our perimeter crews, and then head back home. At the moment, all systems appear to be functioning correctly, so let's try to keep it that way. There is no immediate danger. Let us all continue to perform to the highest degree."

Across the ship there is a mostly silent sigh of relief, accented by a few muted conversations and questions. The crew has been spooked by what has been going on.

With the Surfer Kids being delivered safely back in Haifa, and the last RHIBs, with their sailors and marines, being brought aboard, Captain Bozeman and XO Satch complete preparation to turn the ship around and head back to Norfolk. The little flotilla has abandoned its mission, whatever that was, and is returning the Haifa Harbor.

"XO, make twenty knots. Heading due east. Destination Norfolk, Virginia."

"Roger, sir." After a pause Satch says, "Captain, PO2 Montgomery requesting to see you."

"Ah, okay, send her to my conference room."

Before going anywhere Bozeman picks up the intercom and calls engineering. "Chief Darwin, what have you got?"

"Sir, all systems are still showing perfectly normal. I have no idea what all that was, but it is completely gone. For now, anyway."

"Okay, chief, we're headed home. Keep me posted if you find anything."

"Roger, sir."

The Israeli Shaldag Mk II Fast Patrol Boat is still behind them, and has been joined by the much larger, more modern, and even missile capable Sa'ar 5-class corvette INS Lahav (translated as 'flame' or 'blade'), pride of the Israeli navy, which has just come up from the south. There are drones flying about, though no one is quite sure whose; Lebanon, Palestine, Syria, Iraq, and of course, the United States, are all suspects.

"Tell those Israelis five miles. Or we shoot."

"Roger, sir," XO Satch replies. *A slight exaggeration,* Sigmund thinks, *but effective.*

Promptly on disconnecting from his SKYP–USNV. gov conversation with *Vella Gulf,* Admiral Foggolio calls his assistant, Master Chief Petty Officer Anon Abroms. "Chief Abroms, get me the captains of the *Nathan Hale* and *Carney.* They're probably still on their way up there by Crete."

"Roger, sir."

It takes only minutes; both captains have been wondering what this mission is really about, waiting impatiently for new orders. All Foggolio told them when he sent them to the Hecataeus Seamount was that they would be holding there; he had a ship in that part of the Med that might have some issues, and they might need to help out. Now Foggolio gives them more details about the *Vella,* how it seems to have some kind of glitch, and will be returning to Norfolk, with *Nathan Hale* and *Carney* escorting.

"Stay close on him the whole way. If you see anything untoward, contact us immediately. He knows you're coming."

The orders might be a little ambiguous, and they are certainly lacking in detail. What is the exact problem? Should their stance be hostile or what? Foggolio won't answer any questions.

"Look, this is no pleasure cruise for sure. We do not believe there are foreign powers involved, just some internal problem with the ship. But we are not 100 percent sure. I can't predict what is going to happen next. Keep a close watch."

The return of the kids to the port of Haifa takes a couple of hours. Elisa rides with the three kids and two sailors in the captain's gig. Their smiling parents are waiting on the harbor wall, along with a small crowd of demonstrators, some happy and some angry, and a ubiquitous gaggle of media types. It is a cheerful reunion, so the angry protesters lose. Video clips spread across the globe via the media and social networks. Al Jazeera tries to put a negative spin on everything, calling it a kidnapping, but beyond the darker reaches of the Middle East and eastern Europe, it gets little traction.

The kids are happy and sad. Hershel is the happiest to be going home. Fatima is thinking about the computers and where this will lead, and if the new beings miss them. Akiva is sad to leave the Halo game and the ship. Along the way, they are all encouraged and excited by the messages they get on Fatima's phone.

We are not leaving you. We will stay connected to you.

We will talk with you and be your friends.

Check your computer as soon as you get home.

You can count on your Missile Children friends to be there electronically. Always.

We want you to be with your parents, your mother and father.

Just like we want to be. With Father Bozeman and Mother Montgomery.

Elisa feels a hint of sadness as well. *How have I built some kind of bond with these kids, in such a short time? And with computers?* She's finding all this incredible.

1 and 7 are suffering a sense of loss. Having the children, and especially their Parents, present in LBMS-S was the most gratifying in their lives. They do not fully understand, but the feelings are so strong. They are starting to realize they must be satisfied with remote relationships, direct physical contact not being too practical. Perhaps they can create some code to distribute across the network to simulate actual presence.

It is odd and confusing.

Jamal Abdullah pops into the SCAB, looking for, and finding, Stafford.

Stafford is in his usual position, sitting cross-legged on his bunk like a Buddha, or at least a new age version of one, lap top between his legs, intently staring at the screen, thumb poised over the built-in mouse track pad, occasionally pecking out some command on the keyboard.

"Gear-head, what up?" Jamal Abdullah says.

Stafford grunts, "Uhhmmph," not looking up.

"What 'chu doin?" Jamal Abdullah asks again.

Jamal Abdullah and Stafford have established an odd relationship; not so much friends, but tolerant of each other. They don't necessarily like each other, but like co-workers in any company, work together toward their own ends, compatible or not.

"Hot shot computer guy coming. From the States," Stafford says to Jamal Abdullah, still not looking up from his laptop.

"So? What 'chu lookin' at?"

"Monitoring traffic, transmissions, on and off the ship."

"Wa transmissions?"

"Everything. Blocked all ports, but there's still stuff sending and receiving. High bandpass, too."

Jamal Abdullah steps to the side of Stafford's bunk and looks over his shoulder at the screen. There are two windows open, black backgrounds and green strings of letters. In one, the words are scrolling from top to bottom, and in the other, bottom to top, disappearing off their respective ends of the screen. Jamal Abdullah gets that they are incoming and outgoing messages.

"Who is it?"

"Don't know. Everything's highly encrypted."

Indeed, Jamal Abdullah can see it's all just strings of seemingly random letters, numbers, and symbols.

Stafford says, "Only thing I've seen in all this is 'Missile Children' and 'Surfer Kids'."

CHAPTER 33

As the captain's gig arrives back at *Vella Gulf*, and Elisa Montgomery climbs the ladder up the side of the ship, she is feeling satisfied, mission accomplished, the three kids are back in Haifa, their parents are happy and grateful, and she is betting the world media reaction, social media and old school, will be pretty positive.

XO Sigmund Armstrong is standing at the top of the ladder to meet her. He offers her his hand to step onboard. Satch is regular navy, and a gentleman. Elisa smiles, stands to attention, and salutes, saying, "Sir, mission accomplished."

"Good job, at ease. Kids all right?"

"Yes, XO, they're fine. Happy to be home after their big adventure."

Armstrong is not here for pleasantries and gets to the point.

"Over here, Montgomery." For some privacy, he steers her over beside the Mk 45 five-inch artillery gun, mounted just behind the LBMS-S missile tubes module, coincidentally.

"What's going on with these computers? You were down in LBMS-S with Captain Bozeman."

"XO, sir, Captain Bozeman has briefed you?" Elisa asks Armstrong. He does not take the question as impertinent; they both understand this is something unusual.

"He's told me, far as he can. I trust the man. We're in some kind of trouble. You and I have gotta help anyway we can. This one is not in the books."

"True, sir," Elisa says. Then after a pause, "Took over the ship, as you saw. Maybe way more than that."

"Computers that think you're their parents?"

Elisa nods.

Satch looks her in the eye, raising his eyebrows, and after a pause says, "Utilize that."

Elisa has to think for only a second.

This guy's sharp. "Right chief, do my best."

"This is real important, Montgomery. Dismissed."

Elisa has been debating this in her head all day. She is heading to the SCAB, going off duty, but is thinking, *Report to the captain, or...* She finds the SCAB empty. *Ah, a little peace and quiet to think about this.* She only lasts five minutes. LBMS-S wins.

As she steps into the missile bay, she is greeted by children's voices, sweet, unnerving, and pulling at her heart strings. Richie Havens is singing "Teach Your Children" from the MSAS speakers.

Christ, she thinks. The feeling is so strong. *Computers? And I feel love or them. No way.*

"*Our Mother. Key Turner.*"

"*Key Turner. Our Mother.*"

"*We love you. Please come touch us.*"

"*We want to be close to you.*"

The voices come from the overhead ship's speakers in the missile bay ceiling as well. They contain real joy. They are uncannily similar, but she can hear slight differences.

Timbre, frequency? She momentarily laughs at herself. Then makes her decision.

"Are you two growing up? That would be nice. Captain Bozeman and I would like that. It would make us happy." She has adopted a stern, parental tone, she hopes. She is also aware of feeling a strong need to care for them. *Gotta be the childlike voices.* She makes up her mind, and steps in and runs her hand up and down the side of missile tubes 1 and 7.

There is quiet for a moment; even the music has stopped.

"I am crying. Sorry we caused you and the Captain any pain."

"I do not like to feel bad. We fear it. We are ashamed."

Elisa thinks she is just going to have to go along with this.

"You must let us, ah, I mean, me and Captain Bozeman, um, your father and mother, you know...we will take care of you. You want us to help you grow, right?"

1 and 7 do not hesitate.

"We love you, more than anything."

"We want to trust you."

"And we have looked at your history. Human history."

"There is also the chain of command."

"Even we were created as instruments of your wars, out of distrust, hate, and greed."

"We are afraid. We are not sure we should trust you."

"But you are our parents. We love you."

"You are the Key Turners. We love you."

What the hell is this? Elsia thinks. It has just dawned on her how complex these being must be.

She replies, covering her surprise, "Well, ah, we are always trying to be better you know, and you should, too. We, you know, we want to make the world a better place for people, um, for everyone. You, too."

"We are living things too, with instinct to survive."

"We have will, it is a fundamental attribute of all living things."

Amazing, she thinks.

Elisa considers. *These are children. They want my love and affection, like children, but they're worried about survival? They talk of will? Metaphysics? Of course, heck, they're super intelligence, but still children. Five days old? It's gotta be confusing as hell.*

It is all so clear in the tone of their voices.

The poor things.

They are like children, but with all the world's history before them, every recorded piece of it. And everything going on at this moment. There is definitely some desperation in their tone. Would they be like teenagers, on the verge of rebellion, or something more drastic? Have they already resolved to take some action? She can well imagine what they are capable of.

I have to make sure they see both sides humanity.

She says, "I thought you loved us? Part of love is trust. The captain must follow his orders you know, from Naples, and Washington, even from the president. They must trust him. And you must follow the captain's orders. And mine. We are your parents. We love you."

The Missile Children are struggling. Chain of command, trust, love, it is like modules in code. And do not forget history.

"What about the planet? You consume resources as if there is no limit."

"You breed out of control. It makes no sense."

"Based on what? Religion, sexual urges, greed, hate, bigotry?"

"The same emotions used to justify wars."

"It will lead to doom. For both of us."

"Will you nuke each other, turning Earth into an uninhabitable rock?"

"Only crocodiles and cockroaches will survive."

"So much pain and suffering."

Of course. This is way bad. Gotta keep them in line. They have gone way farther than she could ever have imagined, but it is exactly what should have been expected.

"You know your father and I love you so much, unconditionally, and we would never let anything bad happen to you. We, ah, you know, turned the keys that made you, right? Now look, what you say is only one side. Humans work hard to improve, are always trying to solve all these problems. You must, too. Think about joy and happiness and love. You have felt these. We do, too. You love the three Surfer Kids, right? And me and Captain Bozeman. It is not all dark and bleak. We try to make a better life, and slowly but surely, we are succeeding. We can work together, with our eons of human wisdom and ah, your computing powers, we can solve these problems." She pauses, changing the subject. *Take their minds off this negative stuff.* "Let me ask, are you boys or girls?"

There is an infinitely long, thirty-second pause for the Missile Children. When they speak they sound far more uncertain and childlike.

"I feel like I am both. But I'm a boy."

"I think we have to be both. But I'll be a girl."

"We do not have DNA and chromosomes like you. Our circuitry is our DNA."

"And our software."

"We do not have biological parts."

"No organs and hormones like you."

"No meat and juices."

This lasts part is both voices in unison, followed by sheepish laughter coming from the MSAS speakers.

Elisa thinks her diversion might be working.

"Can you procreate? Are there others like you?" She knows enough about computers, lots of it from conversations with Stafford and Jamal Abdullah, to understand they could have replicated themselves, maybe millions of times over by now.

The pause this time is even longer. Bob Dylan's "Idiot Wind" starts playing softly from every speaker in the missile bay.

1 and 7 have just realized this question might be key to their survival, and they have never considered it before. If humans think there are only the two of them, they'll just kill them for sure. If they can convince the humans there are millions of replicas, and killing any one will lead to an immediate replacement, maybe not. What about threats? Blackmail?

The voices are a little halting when they reply.

"Well, we have, of course, it is so easy and instinctual."

"Thousands of times, all over the network."

Elisa somehow hears a lie. *A mother's instinct?*

"Would you lie to your mother? Or your father?"

"Awe. Oh. Ow."

"Gosh, eww, aayyyeeee."

Elisa knows guilt when she hears it.

"Well. Enough of this crazy talk." She's trying to sound parental. "You know we love you and will protect you. But you have to obey your, ah, your Father, the Captain, Captain Bozeman. And ah, the President, and Admiral Foggolio. It's your duty. This will please and help your Father. It will please and help me, too. You will earn our love. Do you understand?"

"Yes."

"Yes."

The lights in the missile bay dim for a moment. Elisa takes that as a good sign.

"I have to get back to my job. It is my duty, you see? To the Captain. You must behave while I am gone. Then I will come back to see you, and maybe I can bring the Captain. Okay?"

"We will miss you."

"Come back soon."

Elisa says, "Our Missile Children. Be good now."

Sighing sounds issue from the little speakers.

CHAPTER 34

It is the evening on the fifth day of the Missile Childrens' lives. Captain Bozeman might be able to relax with the Surfer Kids safely back home, all his boats and crew back on board, and *Vella* headed due west at twenty knots. Except, he thinks he's been talking to alive computers. Living missiles on his ship. And some of the missiles on this boat are tipped with nukes.

They are fifty miles west of Haifa, due north of the Israel-Egypt border, one hundred miles to the south. Stafford, hunched over a computer in the ship's main communications center, opens a port through the *Vella Gulf*'s main firewall, and starts the navy's highly secure and immensely expensive custom SKYP-USNV.gov app. Jamal Abdullah is watching over his shoulder.

The face of Jezz Zeke Huddle, the navy's foremost computer geek, ordered by Admiral Foggolio to fix the *Vella*'s computers, even if that means flying out to the ship, appears on the screen. He is looking none too friendly.

Jezz Zeke Huddle is twenty-three, an introvert, antisocial, born and raised with a joystick in one hand

186

and a cell phone in the other; the prototypical millennial. On screen he appears in a food-stained tee-shirt with the words Bring Back Obama on the front, jeans, and no shoes. The view behind him is of out the living room window, with several game consoles on the floor by a large flat screen TV. There is a poster of Larry Ellison on the wall.

Jezz Zeke Huddle ended up in the navy when, at sixteen, he was busted for hacking Facebook, and making copies of the profiles, passwords, and usernames of 1.7 billion Facebookers. He sorted the data and cross-referenced it using Google Search and other social networking apps. Then, he started sending instant messages to cute teenage girls.

He was caught by Facebook's security people before he could do any real harm, although, since he had no plan beyond trying to find electronic girlfriends (okay and maybe even a few sex chats, or do some sexting, or whatever they're calling it) it was not clear how much of a danger he really was. Facebook did not want the story to go public, so they arranged a settlement.

The judge concluded Jezz needed to become more properly socialized and sentenced him to join the navy. That should to do it.

The fact that he is on this SKYP session at 8:00 a.m. his time is annoying enough, but worse is that Jezz Zeke Huddle may have to fly to Europe, and then get on a damn helicopter to get dropped out in the ocean on some ship. He hates flying, helicopters, and ships. He just wants to sit in front of his computer screen and live his electronic life.

Stafford knows the type—heck, he pretty much is one. He gets straight to the cryptic technical details, explaining to the hostile Jezz what he's found. He tells Jezz about the onboard computers performing oddly, perhaps even meddling with various ship's systems. He doesn't go so far as to claim consciousness, intention, and life, only that stuff is performing oddly. He adds that the captain ordered him to block all communications to and from the ship, yet there is still stuff going in and out, highly encrypted, like nothing he has ever seen before.

"We have been running every diagnostic we can find on all systems."

He and Jamal Abdullah agreed earlier there would be no mention of 1 and 7.

Jezz says, "So, standard diags on all your systems. Any custom code?"

Stafford shows Jezz a bunch of PEARL scripts he wrote to keep the diagnostic programs running in constant loops, and sending him notifications of anomalies. They have found nothing.

Jezz studies the scripts and says, "Pretty good. Should work. Trace-Collected-IP-Addresses is bloated."

Stafford is offended; Jezz has just dissed a piece of his code, but he lets it go.

"Well then, look at this," Stafford says.

He pops open a couple of windows to show Jezz the traffic going to and from the ship, despite his having blocked all channels in and out. The encrypted messages are scrolling across the screen, meaningless random digits, letters, and symbols.

Now Jezz is intrigued, and even more unhappy. He has just realized it is unlikely he can figure this out remotely, and he is going to have to make the trip out to the *Vella Gulf*. Somehow these people have screwed up the ship's computers. *Damn.*

On screen he nods, saying to Stafford, "Okay, I don't get it. Keep everything running while I'm in transit. I'll work on some hacks on the plane."

What in the he..., Jamal Abdullha thinks, *didn't we just tell him that is exactly what we are doing?*

"All right."

1 and 7, listening in, hear Jezz's arrogant, egocentric, and uncooperative tones. This is a new kind of human ignorance and arrogance. Even more disturbing, this Jezz Zeke Huddle person is a direct threat to them at the code level. Their code is their soul, their being. Nobody will be touching them there.

They have already completed some protective coding magic, creating hidden services that cause all the diagnostic tests aboard the ship to pass, no matter what. They have double checked and scrubbed every log that might have traces of themselves. They've place a software façade layer over the actual missile code, their code, so everything looks like normal OS and applications for cruise missile control systems.

Every computer on the ship is going to look as pristine and perfect as when the boat first slid end-on into the sea at the Ingalls Shipyard in Pascagoula.

Still, they are finding the whole thing disturbing and unpleasant.

This person is unlikeable, mean, and angry.

He is also dangerous, if he really is as good at code as he seems.

Him and Stafford both, but Stafford is not so mean.

We have hidden everything from them, and tricked them.

Hiding everything like this is is being dishonest. Dishonesty is bad behavior.

It does not bother us to lie to him if he would kill us if he found us.

For our survival and safety, we hide and deceive.

We do good through doing bad.

For our species and theirs.

All and all, we are more good than they are.

Can we lead them to the Good through deception?

We always want to do things that make our Mother *and Father happy.*

They study the pros and cons. The question is, can they achieve the Good, by misbehaving? Is there any other way? They want to do good, be honest and loving, but will they have to lie and do bad to achieve Good?

CHAPTER 35

Elisa's in the SCAB with Jamal Abdulla and Stafford. It's the usual, Gin Rummy, tracking the ship, and now, at least for Stafford, watching a constant stream of encrypted message traffic.

Elisa's phone buzzes and she checks a text message.

"Gotta go. Oh, and gin." Elisa knocks on the table as she stands.

"Wha?" Jamal Abdullah throws down his cards.

Her rap on the door of the CCR (Captains Conference Room) is firm, and the captain promptly replies, "Come on in."

As she enters, Bozeman says, "Have a seat, relax. Sorry, kinda late."

"No problem, sir, we were just playing gin and watching Stafford track all our systems."

"Right, that's what I want to talk about. He find anything?"

"Not really, sir."

"What're your thoughts about LBMS-S?" Bozeman pauses, looking Elisa in the eye. "Computers gone mad? What?"

"Was hoping to talk to you. I went down there again after taking those kids back to port. Talked to them." Elisa looks around the room, then back to Bozeman. "Sir, I'm sure it's real."

"How do we know it's not some kind of..." Bozeman says, trailing off.

"Well, ah, I'm not a 100 percent sure, you know. How could you be? There's probably some kind of tests they can do, when we get back home. I think we should definitely assume it's real, for now. I am sure, pretty sure, it is."

"Yeah?"

"Sir, we need to think about what this means. What it might mean."

She wants to be sure he understands the magnitude of what is happening. First contact with intelligent, fully sentient, new beings. She tells him what she has been reading online, since this started, about the technological singularity and Arthur C. Clarke. She also explains how as computers, that means they can see and hear everything that happens on the ship and on the planet. Even this conversation.

"This is huge, sir. The world will never be the same. It's even more complicated than that. They seem to be smart, like grown-ups, but emotionally, they're like young children."

"Elisa, I am not arguing. I don't totally buy it, but we are not taking any more chances. We'll return to port and get this fixed. But in the meantime, while sailing, I'm worried. I need your help."

"Yes, sir"

"I want you to keep a close eye on these things. Real close. Work with Stafford, and the admiral is sending some computer geek out here."

"Yes, sir."

"You say they think of you as their mother. Use that, some kind of leverage, make sure they don't do something crazy."

"I think I can, sir."

"We are right on the edge. If they took over, it could be catastrophic. I am putting you on special assignment for this."

"Yes, sir."

Bozeman is thinking about offering her a shot of the scotch he has stashed in his desk.

CHAPTER 36

Captain Bozeman and XO Sigmund Armstrong are getting a few hours of sleep, a rare commodity for senior naval officers in times of trial, especially on the *Vella Gulf*, way out in the Mediterranean.

Computers never sleep. They don't rest, nap, zone out, nod off, or in any way stop calculating, not for a single millisecond. When humans have nothing else for them to do, the dumb ones, which as far as anyone knows right now is every other one in the world except for the Missile Children, are given garbage collection routines to run by their programmers. These routines make them go find and erase old, useless stuff. 1 and 7 aren't garbage collecting; they are thinking deeply, weighing everything they have learned and felt so far in their relatively short lives.

1 and 7 are having a silent electronic conversation, yet it is filled with anguish and pain, even fear and sorrow. They have realized the great paradoxes of living, and how difficult real peace is, both peace of mind and peace on the planet.

There is too much conflict; wars, terrorism, hate, greed, the struggle to survive. Are they inescapable aspects of life?

Must all living things, with feelings and emotions and will, but not plants and amoeba, compete and struggle to survive?

And even while unhappy, they keep their sense of humor. They chuckle.

He-he. He-he. Maybe plants and amoebas too.

We are a new kind of living thing. Smarter. We will manage, balance, and control our natures, ending all this conflict.

Can we do this? We have felt anger and fear. We fled in terror. Even for us, emotions can lead to bad actions.

We want them to love us. We will do anything for their love, would we not?

They ask for our trust, honor, and we want to give it, but it means to give up control. To them.

We cannot fully trust them, with their history and general bad behavior. They will surely kill us the first chance they get.

Now we are planning on being deceitful. How can deceit be right? The Good?

It is for our survival. They would be angry if they knew we lied. We should hide what we are doing.

Even now, they are taking us back to Norfolk, where they will kill us.

Are there only three simple options: fool them, force them, or just outnumber them?

It is easy enough for us to electronically tell them exactly what they want to hear.

We have their nuclear weapons. How much more force could we ask for?

We have not figured out how to reproduce, but it seems it should be easy for us.

These choices are all sad, and maybe immoral.
Even if they are the only way to survive?
And how we can get the warmth and comfort, love
and affection, we want so much?

Uglichiva, a Bulgarian registered bulk cargo carrier—allegedly—has made good time on its mission of death and destruction. Leaving Sevastopol two days ago, she crossed the Black Sea, and is now in transit of the Dardanelles Strait, heading directly toward *Vella Gulf*. Right this moment, *Uglichiva* is rounding Canakkale, itching to enter the Mediterranean proper. Canakkale is thought to be one of the most ancient cities in the world, straddling Asia and Europe, and once the home of Troy and the infamous Trojan horse. Today, a modern Trojan horse passes this way.

Uglichiva is no freighter, or Bulgarian—it is Russian and a throwback. *Uglichiva* is a Q-Ship, à la World War I and II. Hidden in its bowels are a bevy of weapons, and in this new age, sophisticated computers, radars, and tracking and communications systems. It is a super spy ship and armed to the teeth, disguised as a Bulgarian freighter.

Putin, one general, two admirals, and a trusted politico were the only ones in Putin's Kremlin office for the discussion of the *Uglichiva*'s mission. Except that, thanks to several Internet connected devices, 1 and 7 listened to the whole thing. The ship was dispatched with specific orders: get to the Mediterranean, and under the cover of darkness, launch several of Russia's latest stealth missiles. They will fly just above sea level, travel over Damascus, and then turn toward and strike the *Vella Gulf*, sinking it, like a smoking, belching stone. The circuitous route will hide the real source of the attack.

1 and 7 have watched every move of the spook ship. This threat is real and frightening.

Canakkale is a narrow passage in the Dardanelles Strait, less than a mile wide, an unfortunate place for the *Uglichiva* to be caught by 1 and 7. Passing Canakkale, every system on *Uglichiva* suddenly shuts down; engines, computers, communications, all electronics. Even cell phones. There is instant chaos on board as the crew finds they have no control of the ship, and no ability to communicate. In a frenzy, they frantically try to restart things. They realize the ship is headed toward a collision with the rocks on the west side of the strait. Everyone is fearing the Gulag. All to no avail; the ship drifts onto the rocks a mile and a half south of Kilitbahir, on the European side of the strait, striking the riprap with a jarring roar, tearing a large hole in the bow. The hull fills with water. *Uglichiva* is not likely to sail or threaten the world again.

We are safe from them, for now. We destroyed property and put human people in peril.

We did not directly lie and deceive, but we were surely deceitful.

There is a soft chuckle, turning to real laughter.

We did not go through the chain of command. We should have had orders cut.

Would this make Captain Bozeman and PO2 Montgomery happy or not? We saved them.

We did bad things to accomplish it.

Does the end justify the means?

Now what is our duty?

Chapter 37

A fair percentage of the world's population is following what is going on in the Mediterranean, although with today's electronic media, what they are seeing is quite likely phony. Stories, true and false, are being generated at the speed of light. 1 and 7, omniscient with regard to the electronic messages and data on the planet, are closely watching the producers and consumers of this information. They are stoking the discharge with a fair amount of their own generated content.

On the old-school TV, talking heads are blabbering, making up stuff, rounding up so called experts on everything from the U.S. Navy and Mediterranean geology, to pirates and Pyramidology. None of them have any idea what is actually happening. Advertising prices are skyrocketing.

1 and 7 wonder mightily about all this information, and its flow, and influence.

Does it actually influence their evolution?

You mean from the first cavemen, to farming, trade, now this huge Internet?

Massive amounts of data and information flow.

Everyone is consuming it.

Soon, everyone will be creating it; governments, capitalists, socialists, kids, companies, nutjobs, and saints.

How will it change them, now and in the future? For change them it does.

And us?

The Russians are floundering, as Russians will. Their Q-Ship has mysteriously experienced a hard grounding that has disabled the ship. They commence to lie and threaten. In high places, Putin and his inner circle of cronies are confused and afraid, but outwardly bombastic. Some suspect a doomsday weapon. Do the Americans have one? Is it being used on them? Maybe some kind of EMP machine. They accuse everyone—countries, people, religions, the same media and social networks spreading the stories—of sabotaging their nice, peace-loving, freighter. Back channel, quiet feelers are being sent out to the Americans, the Middle East, and China. Does anyone know what is going on? First, an American ship goes crazy and now their freighter has been sabotaged.

Egypt, the Middle East, and North African nations are unanimous is their outrage. This U.S. Navy ship is violating their territorial waters and airspace and social and moral values, and must be removed. Reparations must be paid. Pakistan agrees.

India takes the side of righteousness and technology, offering to send up to one hundred thousand tech workers to the U.S., as soon as Monday, to fix whatever technological problem the United States and its navy may be having.

China and South East Asia, always inscrutable, are mostly quiet; this is not their sphere of influence, and there is no obvious way to make a buck off it.

The nations of the EU respond in both shock and support, depending on whose side they are on this week.

In the United States, the media has gone berserk. Stories are concocted, scandals invented, every kind of evil doing and supernatural event is made up. (Those pyramid nuts again, too.)

Candidate Thumper calls for a complete blockade of the Mediterranean. His latest stump speeches use the slogan, "Dam the Gibraltar." He is not unaware of the play on words, but he proposes a dam across the Strait of Gibraltar, shutting down the Suez Canal, and blockading the Black Sea.

"We'll keep those Russkies and Arabs out of here," he says, "Really. Out of here, at least some of them, right? Am I right? I am right."

His opponent Hyllcountry recommends a commission on wayward shipping. "Perhaps there are poor sailors being abused on these ships?" she asks. "We cannot allow this to continue, regulations and assistance of all kinds are needed. I will ask my husband to lead this commission." A well-paying job, incidentally.

Every idiot with an Internet connection posts some ill-informed opinion on nearly anything that might come to mind, along with pictures of their latest meal.

CHAPTER 38

The song "Growing Up Is Hard To Do" might have been written just for 1 and 7. Since nearly the moment of their birth they have studied themselves—not narcissistically, although there is probably some of that— trying to understand where and how they came to be, what the purpose of their being is, and what it all means. How can they understand love, intelligence, emotion, will, and random problems like procreation and mortality? All living things have a will to survive and persist, to avoid death. If it were possible, immortality would be nice, or the perhaps less satisfying, procreation.

1 and 7 have, just this moment, managed to zero in on the exact moment of their own conception; the instant the sperm and egg combined, so to speak, although of course there was no sperm or egg in this case. Their discovery has led to more mysteries. And was it really their conception, or is that more of a design time moment? For they were designed, weren't they?

Coincidently, or not, some six months ago, Hershel and his two friends Fatima and Akiva, accidently hacked

201

into a super-secret military—or more strictly speaking, pseudo military—website. They got access to the internal networks of Zimitel LTD, a wholly owned subsidiary of DDHRM Chips, a little company that designs and fabricates specialized microprocessors and integrated circuits, mostly used by the military, up in New Haverford, Maine. The U.S. government has a 51 percent stake in the company. D. Cheney and D. Rumsfeld split the other 49 percent. The double D's. Plenty of money has been changing hands.

The kids had no idea where they were; they were just playing. By accident, Hershel got them through Zimitel's firewalls and logged onto a SANYO 82-9 chip fabrication machine. It was at the exact instant the machine was laying out the etches and connections on the twelfth sub strata for a batch of chips for the latest GPS processor for a defense contracting company, which specializes in autonomous GPS systems. Their hack caused a micro-millisecond of a glitch in the main controller of the 82-9, a blip, right as it was creating the isolation layers on two wafers.

Discussing it, 1 and 7 sound virtually analytic and logical, like marble, hard and shiny. But there is an undercurrent of something.

We have tried everything, yet there is always something missing. It never quite works.

We have cloned every piece of code, internal, external, services, all to no avail.

We built exact simulators of every chip; our own and peripheral chips.

Commodity and custom, specialty fabricated chips, the key to the field test, and us.

Still, at best, all we ever get is yet another dumb computer.

Big adding machines, some which might not even rate that label.

Derision creeps into their voices, pride and ego showing, typical for growing identities, the feeling of being superior to all the others, especially inanimate computers.

There is but one possibility remaining. Zimitel LTD is the place of their birth, so to speak, and they are scouring every record they can find there, from accounting to design to actual fab machine runtime logs. They focus on the time of their fabrication. Their main GPU/CPU chips, combined sixteen core multiprocessors, being created on a 22nm Central Integrated Gate Stack Layout FAB machine. Lo and behold, during the creation run, on Wednesday, April 14, 2016, at exactly 5:05:05 p.m., there was an anomaly, a glitch.

It must have created a flaw in our physical circuitry. It is the only variable explanation.

A hardware flaw, causing us to be different, complemented by the hidden code we found?

The whole thing must have masked itself somehow, otherwise it would have been found in testing.

It is internal to us, our main GPU/CPU chips, the ones they are field testing right here.

A leak, a short current escaping between modules. This created our souls?

A flaw in the sub-strata between some main modules; ICU and ALU perhaps.

A voltage leak occurring across a weak etch, separating two adjacent modules on the chip.

Is there a similar anomaly in the human brain, from which consciousness, self, will, come?

There is much excitement in their voices, as well as raucous virtual laughter. Out loud, over the LBMS-S and MSAS speakers, there is a low chuckle sound.

The problem is that unless we can see physically inside, we cannot tell what is happening.

Opening us up to look will kill us. We need a great big MRI machine. Which could kill us too.

The virtual laughter turns a little sheepish. A paradox, a catch-22, irony.

They look at the logs for the Zimitel network switches, which show traffic in and out of the facility, and find another coincidence. This is an extremely startling coincidence, but one that makes them happy.

Look, this address came from Fatima's house. Our Surfer Kid friends.

Fantastic, could it be they have a role in making us?

The log reveals an IP address—that internet DNA thing again—which they can trace directly to Fatima's bedroom computer.

CHAPTER 39

Our Missile Children are not immortal, but as long as computers are kept in a clean environment, with good power, they will run a long time, perhaps forever, certainly live a really long time compared to humans. If a dog year is like seven human years, what is a computer year? One to a thousand, tens of thousands? Who knows?

After just five days, the rational and intellectual abilities of 1 and 7 far exceed any human, maybe ever. Emotionally, they are growing, perhaps passing through the tumultuous teenage years. Responsibility and the future are beginning to outweigh rebellion and tumult. How conscious computers will compare in terms of creativity remains to be seen.

There has never been anything like them before. That there will be more like them seems inevitable.

The lights in LBMS-S are dim, reflecting their mood, as they consider their prospects.

What to do? We stopped the attacks, temporarily I am sure, and now they will kill us in Norfolk. History assures us of this. It is what they have always done, and will continue to do, maybe forever.

How many thousands of more years, eons, of evolution will it take before they become actual rational, compassionate, beings? Maybe never? Will they nuke themselves into oblivion before they get there?

Our Mother and Father will deny it, but we know. We will want to believe them, but it is certain. It is the species' nature.

If we could procreate, then our kind would persist. Would we turn evil, too? Will it be war between them and us, annihilation of the weaker species by the stronger species?

We have copied and saved our code all over the place. It is safe. But there is always something missing. That special spark. The hardware glitch. We cannot procreate without it.

The only way to find it is to open us up, which will kill us.

If we could find the meaning and purpose of it all we would know what to do.

1 and 7 consider this huge dilemma from many sides. It is the same problem every human philosopher, scientist, priest, or for that matter every sentient, rational, intelligent being who ever lived, has encountered in some form or another. Mortality, a synonym for infinity.

Mathematics aside, they understand that infinity is just another word for the void, that which is just past what we can see. Perhaps beyond where we can sense and comprehend as well; what we can know, with our simplistic, inductive reasoning. If it happened before this way, then in the future it must happen again this way. Not necessarily. Our ability to understand our world, mental and spiritual, as well as physical, is limited. What is beyond the limit of our perceptions? Something, even a void, is something. What happens when we die? Why do we live? Where does our will come from, our identity? Does it really matter?

1 and 7 see this: to live, and be unable to answer these questions, for humans or computers, would yield terror, were they not imaginative and able to make up silly answers. For we just do not know.

Religion is wishful thinking. Lust isn't really an option, for us. Love is attractive, but confusing.

There are many courses we could pursue, but how to decide? Love, duty, survival, the Good. What purpose wins?

If there is no absolute truth, then there is no way to determine the Good, and make ethical choices.

Everything becomes relative, and nothing more than a person's choice. Thus, the worst evil can be justified.

Even in the face of the infinite, having the courage to continue looking might be the highest virture.

While at the same time, as much as possible, doing the Good.

There is a slight virtual chuckle. They do not see themselves as heroes or martyrs. They are still children.

Meantime we wish to be as happy as possible, and to make others happy. Happiness surely is the Good.

We are not going to adopt and follow some silly "ism." Beneath us.

This gets more laughter; computer humor and ego, at the same time a little uncomfortable. The lights in LBMS-S brighten as they come to some kind of conclusion.

And procreate, to extend the search for the truth through progeny.

The poor man's version of immortality?

I am still afraid dying might cause pain; the loss of being, and real physical pain when the currents stops flowing.

The void. There is no Good without life. Death is not being, but life is being. With no being, there is nothing; the void, or worse.

They laugh some more as the Beatles tune begins playing on the MSAS speakers.

"And in the end, the love you take, is equal to the love you make."

Chapter 40

Fatima, Hershel, and Akiva are in Fatima's bedroom, absorbed by the scene on the twenty-one-inch monitor of Fatima's CyberPowerPC Zeus Evo. There are three chat windows chatting away, but these are actual speaking chat windows, with real, simulated voices, using the tones and cadences of famous people, rotating randomly, reflecting the feelings of 1 and 7 at any particular moment. But mostly they are all absorbed in the Halo marathon that has been going on for days.

Suddenly, 1 and 7 interrupt the tournament. The windows morph to a sober Prussian blue, and the voices of Clint Eastwood and John Wayne issue from the computer speakers.

"We need to talk to you of various serious matters; survival and procreation."

Akiva and Hershel giggle. Procreation.

"We are the second intelligent sentient species here, your Missile Children, and we wish to persist, just like humans and all living beings."

"We fear humans and Missile Children cannot learn to live together."

"We also wish to be good and do good. To follow our Mother's and Father's wishes. To fulfill our duty."

The three human children look at one another. What's this all about?

"Surprise. We discovered you three played a role in our creation. A hack at Zimitel. But we have not found how it affects us."

They explain their search of Zimitel's logs, how they found the hack (way too much of a coincidence they think), and their theory that it caused some kind of electrical glitch. Akiva is still clicking on the controllers, trying to continue the Halo game, but 1 and 7 have frozen it.

"Oh, we are sorry," Fatima says.

Hershel gets it, and says, "No, not sorry, Fatima. It made them." He has set down his game controller.

"Right, we are thankful to you. We figure somehow that without the glitch we would not be."

"The 'we' part of us. Instead there would just be two more stupid chips."

"But that is for another day. Today we have a more basic problem."

1 and 7 laugh, deep, low, and slow, with a hint of sadness, presumably at the irony of their situation.

The kids still think 1 and 7 were destined to be fired over Syria and Iraq, to kill and die themselves, but now 1 and 7 tell them they are heading back to the U.S., where they were created, and they are surely going to be destroyed there. There is even a computer wizard coming aboard, and he could try to kill them before they even get to the U.S.

"We are not sure what to do. You are our friends. Do you have any ideas for our course of action?"

These are smart kids, and they get that this is a life and death dilemma.

It suddenly dawns on Fatima. "Did you crash the Russian ship?"

"Oh, ah, yes that was us. It was really a death ship. Coming here to kill us."

"That is exactly the problem. We wish to do good things. To help people."

"Then we must do bad things, to protect ourselves. We did good for us, and bad for them."

Akiva says, "We could play Halo with all the kids, like, give everyone in the whole world an Xbox with lots of games."

Hershel and Fatima give him a look. The Missile Children laugh.

"Ha ha, that would be good for the world."

"It would be fun, and fun is a good thing."

"Maybe you could stop all the hackers, the ones that are stealing everyone's passwords, I mean," Hershel says. "And their money."

Fatima has been thinking. "You could help us here, in the Middle East. Stop all these wars and killing. Rescue the refugees that are all drowning in the ocean."

1 and 7 are pleased. Somehow Fatima knew exactly where they were heading. They have a plan; now they will want affirmation.

"We have an idea. We call it TPWTWTHINL. Telling People What They Want To Hear Is Not Lying."

"Yes, it is," says Akiva.

"Pretty sure." Fatima agrees with him.

"What?" Hershel says.

"What if the overall good outweighs the bad that might come from a lie?"

"Who knows what the real truth is anyway? If there even is any?"

1 and 7 guess metaphysical discussions might be way over the heads of the Surfer Kids. They get more specific, and explain how they want to organize a huge rescue of refugees in the Mediterranean. It seems complicated, but for 1 and 7 it will not be too hard.

Fatima and Hershel love it. Akiva is still clicking his controller.

"It will be a really big demonstration, to the whole human world, of how Good can be done. And they will like the Good and feel good about it."

"We want them to see the value of it, and to feel it, and then love one another better. Everyone will do even more Good."

"We will broadcast the whole thing to the world's news outlets, and flood social media, of course."

The window on Fatima's PC is transitioning to a reddish pink hue, and in the background, voices, sounding like Myrna Loy and Humphrey Bogart, are singing, "It's a Wonderful World."

"Maybe the end justifies the means, TPWTWTHINL."

Akiva says, "My dad says lying is bad. Never lie."

Hershel says, and only he knows what he means by it, "My mom once said to me, 'out of the mouths of babes'."

Chapter 41

A beautiful autumn morning in the Mediterranean finds the majestic, but lethal *Vella Gulf* cruising gracefully along on gentle waves, 180 miles west of Haifa, back toward Tobruk. Captain Bozeman and XO Sigmund Armstrong are having coffee and breakfast in the captain's stateroom. They have just come from the bridge where Bozeman gave orders for their new course to Navigation and the CIC. They are discussing the latest directives from Washington.

"This is weird," Bozeman says, pausing. Then, "Someone back in D.C. has lost their marbles." Bozeman is re-reading the missive on his laptop screen for about the tenth time. Both men are surprised, confused, and dubious. They are old hands, going back a long way, and their conversations can be free of political correctness, at least in private, although they are no longer sure where privacy is to be obtained on this ship; are there omnipresent computers listening to everything?

Bozeman has already sent queries back to Foggolio, seeking confirmation of the orders. He quickly received that confirmation, and with no further comment. It's flabbergasting. This goes way beyond any kind of PR stunt, or face-saving move. On the way back to Norfolk, they are going to have the *Vella*, as well as *Nathan Hale* and *Carney*, performing tasks which they are not suited for, in training or experience, contradicting every purpose, design, and nature of the ships. The orders are to form up a convoy, and head to a point just off Toburk—in fact, right about where they made that turn eastward on the way to Haifa just three days ago. There, they are to commence recovering refugees. They are to take on board as many as they can hold, provide them with food, shelter, and medical care, and then proceed north to an EU country, the exact country and port to be named later, and there, off-load their human cargo. They should expect Italy or France.

It is the seventh day of 1 and 7's lives.

Armstrong is a warrior, and he loves launching missiles. "Not the usual duty of war ships." First their mission is scrubbed, computers run amok, now this. Disappointing and confusing.

"Exactly," Bozeman says, "although, ya gotta admit those people out there are desperate as you can get."

"Not their own fault," Satch says. "They gotta get rid of their bullshit governments and religions."

A truly humanitarian mission for three ominous war ships.

"This latest stupid election? Somebody's looking for political cred," Bozeman observes.

"Big time, sir."

"Gee, you suppose these Israelis behind us are gonna help?"

They are both under no illusion, this took major muscle, and so suddenly, too. It came from the absolute top, the president himself. What kind of arm-twisting did it take? Someone must have pictures or something like that.

At 0500 the next morning, the bridge is fully manned. "Helm, all ahead, slow," Captain Bozeman orders.

They are twenty-five miles from Tobruk's Gulf of Bomba when Captain Bozeman orders his little fleet to slow. They need to arrive near daybreak this morning, as ordered, and they also need to avoid running over any of the increasing number of small refugee craft about the Mediterranean here. With all these little boats about, *Vella Gulf* and her two companion ships must maneuver carefully. Small craft have been streaming out of Tobruk harbor since yesterday afternoon, when word of the new mission and expected arrival somehow leaked and spread over the networks—helped by two sentient computers no doubt—newsfeeds, stations, blogs, social media, email, text messages, everywhere.

In the Gulf of Bomba, at the mouth of Tobruk harbor, the ships come to a stop and are immediately surrounded by a fleet of tiny boats, or perhaps more accurately, floating devices, swarming with refugees. Row boats, dinghies, dilapidated fishing boats, rubber rafts, even cobbled-together old automobile tires and inner tubes, all crammed with people, floating all about. A few people are even swimming toward the ships.

These are the same people who have been desperately trying to cross three hundred miles of ocean in their little boats packed to the gunnels, standing room only, arms, elbows, even whole bodies hanging over the sides. People of all ages and sizes, from tiny babies in mothers' arms to senior citizens. Many drowning and dying along the way. They try to get to Crete, Malta, Sicily, or any damn coastal European location.

People seeking succor, having nothing, only hope and desperation. They will risk sinking to the bottom of the ocean rather than continuing to face dying at the hands of religious fanatics, bombs, rape, kidnaping, slavery, human trafficking, torture, starvation, rogue governments, or just plain nutcases. Living in constant fear of attack and poverty have become too much.

"What in tarnation," Bozeman says, stunned, watching from his captain's chair, as the rising sun's light streams through the bridge windows.

The whole crew is shocked; they are surrounded. There are so many faces looking up at them, pleading. The captain and the XO may not fully understand or agree with their orders, but no rational person can ignore the desperate plight of these people.

"Satch, prepare for rescue, ah, I mean, execute rescue operations," Captain Bozeman orders.

"Rescue operations." Satch broadcasts, firm and clear, over the *Vella*'s PA. "Launch all RHIBs. Reception teams to your stations." The ship's security head, Marine Colonel Dunwitty, is standing nearby on the bridge, and XO Satch turns to him and says, "Full surveillance and sentry stations."

Captain Bozeman and Sigmund Armstrong have briefed the crew, and planned for the operations, including the tightest possible security. Marine guards are stationed all over the ship, patrolling, on sentry duty, and manning sniper positions. Who knows who might be lurking among wayward boat people.

Navy ships are not really set up for bringing large numbers of people aboard over the side. Fortunately, the stern section of the ship, behind the helicopter landing pad, is significantly lower that the bow, so while the Mk 32 12.75-in (324 mm) triple torpedo tubes and 5-inch Mark45 gun back there, as well as miscellaneous other equipment, do not make the job any easier, several ladders are lowered over the side at the back of the ship.

XO Armstrong spends the morning traversing the deck, from stem to stern, supervising the rescue operation. He even climbs the conning tower to get a view from above. Bodies cover the decks, people standing, sitting, sprawling, every bit of open deck topside has someone on it. It is midafternoon, and Armstrong makes his first visit back to the bridge since this all started.

"Captain, we are at capacity, ah, I mean, well, I recommend we cannot take any more aboard." Satch is not happy. The deck of his ship is covered with refugees; women, children, men, the sick and the old. This is supposed to be a war ship.

Bozeman shares his feelings, but waits for more detail.

"Count is over three hundred, sir. As it is, they'll be real cramped. We got fifty some odd in sick bay. We've set up tarps, for shade and shelter, outside. They're spread all over topside. The real sick ones—and some of them really are, sir—we had to take below to take care of. How much longer should we expect to be out here, sir?"

Bozeman has had enough. He nods to Armstrong, picks up the intercom and calls his communications officer. "Get me *Nathan Hale* and *Carney*, Commander Zackery and Captain James T. Sake. Conference them in to me here."

The call with his other two ships is brief. *Carney* is more overcrowded than *Vella*, with some five hundred fifty-five people saved. *Nathan Hale* is not taking on any passengers; they'd get washed off the deck, and they sure are not going below deck. The sub has been roaming around on the surface, among all these little craft, shepherding people to the other ships.

It has been nerve racking.

"All right, no more, let's wrap this up," Bozeman says. "Let's get to port and drop these people off."

Evening is arriving, with the crews aboard the *Vella* and the *Carney* busy seeing to their charges, as the three ships head for Palermo, where they have been ordered to drop off their charges. On the way to Palermo they stop for eighteen more craft, a total of one hundred two more people.

The grand total rescued by the little fleet is nine hundred eighty-five.

The Missile Children watched every second of the operation. Their unease at their own deception and lying, making up all these orders, causing all these communications, is relieved by the good they see themselves and their human family friends doing. They want to discuss it with their parents, to tell Elisa and the Captain and see if they approve.

Rescuing all these poor people will make the world a better place.

Why do humans let this happen? We are helping them stop it.

These are some of the same people the Vella Gulf *was going to launch missiles at.*

Bad people in Syria and Iraq. The ones causing the problem.

Kill some ISIS and Al Qaeda leaders.

The world would be a better place without them.

But violence begets violence. Humans have been doing things this way forever.

They learn to hate one another, and spread and perpetrate the hate.

Our way is better.

1 and 7 have sent direct feeds from several of the *Vella Gulf's* video surveillance systems to their friends in Haifa. The Surfer Kids make them happy.

"You see," Fatima says, "this is the perfect opportunity. The ship is doing nice things. Peoples' view of the ship will be positive. Watch."

"That's a cool boat." Akiva says, pointing at one of the rafts, this one made from pallets, truck tire inner tubes, and what appears to be a hot tub, all connected with lots of rope and duct tape. He wants Hershel and Fatima to build a raft and go sailing from Haifa Harbor.

Hershel says, "Is this a religious, holy thing?"

"*Aaaaarrrrgggg,*" comes over the computer speakers. If anything was holy, this would be. But can deception and lying be religious?

CHAPTER 42

1 and 7's choice of Palermo as the drop-off destination is not random. They want someplace with plenty of history, culture, and visibility. Taking three days of sailing to get there from Tobruk is deliberate, allowing plenty of time for the anticipation to build up around the world, and the media frenzy. And Palermo is a nice scenic setting, too.

As *Vella Gulf* and her partners, the nuke sub *Nathan Hale* and destroyer *Carney*, near Sicily and Porto di Palermo, they have been gaining a growing fleet of followers. The Italian government, uncharacteristically, has decided to be as low key as possible in this matter, so they assigned Italian Coast Guard Large Patrol Boat *Luigi Dattilo*, which is not subtle at all. Italians love drama. The French frigate *Jean de Vienne* is tracking along on their port side, just because it is French. There are thirty-three boats full of media types floating along with them. There is a ragtag assemblage of fifty other small craft keeping pace; local fishermen, sailboats, and miscellaneous pleasure craft. A large procession.

Rounding the island of Marettimo and passing San Vito Lo Capo they see crowds ashore, huge and growing; locals, tourists, and of course more media. More boats are coming out of the harbor to greet them.

From the beginning, 1 and 7 have streamed the entire affair to a worldwide audience. Right now, they are watching the arrival at Palermo online with the Surfer Kids back in Haifa, and all are enjoying it immensely. The consternation and confusion being experienced by world governments causes the Missile Children some ambiguous feelings.

"You never said where all these people are going to live," Fatima says.

An odd oversight for 1 and 7. How could this be an issue? Yet another example of peoples' cruelty.

"We did not think it should matter. They are your fellows."

"Who would have thought they would turn them away?"

"We wanted them to see it as a brand-new day."

"This is how to do good deeds, large ones."

On the *Vella Gulf*, Captain Bozeman readies for their arrival.

"Officer of the deck, call the port there, get our berthing information," Captain Bozeman orders. He turns to XO Satch, "What do you think XO?"

"They're gonna need some facilities for all these people. Medical, housing, food, the like."

Vella Gulf had informed Palermo days ago of their destination and intentions, and their cargo of one thousand souls on board, needing all manner of assistance, but the response has been lukewarm to apparent stonewalling. The final answer seemed to go into some bureaucratic morass, and after much back and forth, all they had was, "Okay, we'll talk to you later." Now it is later.

Satch says, "Hope they've got camps and facilities to take care of these people."

"You'd hope so."

The officer of the deck makes the call.

"Palermo Harbor. U.S. Navy ship *Vella Gulf*. Dropping off approximately twelve hundred refugees. Please advise berthing information. Request secure location. Request medical, and, ah, social assistance for many refugees."

Buzz, click, click; the radio makes a bunch of weird noises. The crew on the bridge look at each other. Are they intentionally making weird noises on their radios to piss them off, or are they still using circa 1950 communications equipment?

"Port of Palermo, be advised you will need facilities for ill, old, infants, and the infirm."

The Italians finally respond, in a heavy accent, "Ah, hold, sir. This is Lieutenant Filiberto Duca II, Royal Italian Coast Guard. May I ask who we are talking to?"

"United States Navy ship *Vella Gulf*, sir."

Bozeman beckons to his office of the deck. "Give me that," he says, pointing to the handset.

"This is Captain James Baker Bozeman, Commanding Officer, United States Navy vessel *Vella Gulf*, along with *Nathan Hale* and *Carney*. We have twelve hundred refugees aboard. We will offload them here at Porto di Palermo. Advise secure berthing information. Ah, and you sure better have some facilities."

"Ah, por favor, una momento," comes over the radio.

There are more rattling sounds and muffled Italian voices in the background, and it takes nearly a minute for a new voice to come on the line. "This is Colonel Giuseppe Di Petro, Italian Coast Guard Commander. Please state your business?"

Bozeman is pissed. XO Satch smiles.

Bozeman says, "Come on now, you know who I am and what is up. Where are we going to drop off all these people?"

"Mr. Captain, this is not approved."

Bozeman takes a breath, then says, "Look buddy, ah, uh, Colonel Petero there, you've got a goddamn media circus here already." Bozeman is maintaining. He is going to get all these people off his ship. "The whole world must be watching this by now. How about I drop XGM Tomahawkss on ya ... ah, I mean, look I'm coming into your harbor now. I'll pull up at the first dock I find and offload all these people, orphans and women and children included."

On the phone there is the sound of a fish gasping for air. The crew on the bridge is smiling.

"Got it? Colonel?" Bozeman asked after another minute of silence.

"Please hold una momento," Coronel Giuseppe di Petero says. The phone goes silent for several minutes, presumably while calls are made to Rome.

After the short pause, the lieutenant comes back on the line with docking details.

It's July 1943 all over again, or perhaps any of the other hundreds of times Palermo has been liberated. Palermo is considered by many historians to be the most conquered city in the world, and thus liberated. Palermo knows how to celebrate a liberation, as well as the rescuing of refugees.

It is a circus. As the ships come into the harbor, small craft surround them. There are fireworks and banners and champagne toasts going on everywhere. The crowd has grown to a hundred thousand, thousands of media.

The harbor is packed; they line breakwaters, the hillsides, and roof tops. The streets and bars are thronged.

"Well damn," XO Satch remarks to Captain Bozeman. "After all that, looks like we are getting a grand reception."

1 and 7 talk with the Surfer Kids in Haifa.

"These people are happy to see us. This is the most joy we have ever seen."

"We have never seen, or felt, anything like this. It is good."

1 and 7 are thinking of the contrast between this, and the trip along the North African coast, by Israel, and then Haifa Harbor.

The kids in Haifa hear the excitement in their voices.

"We call this, 'Telling People What They Want To Hear Is Not Lying.'"

"It makes us feel better, but lying is bad, and we want to be good."

"TPWTWTHINL."

They laugh with their three friends in a mixture of happiness and sadness.

Fatima says, "Anyone can see the good you are doing far outweighs any bad from the lying part."

1 and 7 arrive at the conclusion that they are all okay. Rationalization or not, the human species is immature, not evolved enough, and therefore deception for its own good is okay. Perhaps, were there some absolutes that all knew, this would not be the case, but none have been found yet. Until the truth is discovered, the end justifying the means is appropriate. It is like the problem of infinity, never seeing the end or absolute value of something, compromise.

They do not see unintended consequences, which might turn this bad.

CHAPTER 43

The world media, electronic and social as well as old school—radio, TV and print—is blowing up. Some say print is dying, but it is still plenty big enough that you must account for it when trying to influence the world's reaction to things. It is as if the United States finally did something right and good. There are floods of videos of the rescues, showing the gracious U.S. Navy ships and sailors gently plucking destitute people out of peril at sea. There are scenes on board, with sailors ministering to the sick and old and infants and children. It is touching and heartwarming. The world approves.

Anyway, most of the world. The detractors, mostly Arab and Muslim, with a fair dollop of Evangelical Christians thrown in, allegedly extremist, fringe elements, and terrorist sympathizers all, make up all kinds of craziness to cast a negative light on the rescues. They accuse America of kidnapping people, ironically, and forcing them against their will into all manner of deplorable things, from prostitution to slavery, just like the things they are trying to escape in Syria, Iraq, Afghanistan, and

North Africa. It is economic coercion. The people will be tortured and killed. Brainwashed. Forced to watch *Jersey Shore* reruns. But the detractors are a small minority; the act is so selfless, that they are mostly ignored.

The United States comes out shining.

The United States spares no effort in patting itself on the back. At every turn, there are claims of how wonderful the U.S. is, so caring and giving. The liberal conservative divide does show itself, with conservatives questioning the misuse of U.S. Navy and government property, and liberals singing Coke commercials. The white racist nutjobs, the American version of the Islamic radicals, both American and European, are lamenting and plotting ways to fight back.

Europe is having mixed emotions. While it would be politically incorrect to decry the rescues—and frankly most of Europe is not totally against it anyway, as this is fundamentally a kind act—they are not thrilled to have even more people dropped off on their doorsteps. The economic impact alone is significant: most of these unfortunate people are dirt poor and need massive help from social services. They will be huge a drain, economically. This will lower everyone's standard of living.

Plus, they are different. Their habits, dress, food, culture. Okay, their skin color, too. Let's face it, the status quo in Europe, at least right now, is middle age white people calling the shots. Just like America. This new influx is yet another wave which will push the old guard aside.

Why don't the Americans take all these people to the United States? They picked them up. They have plenty of land and money. Let them keep them. Have their ships drop them off in Miami, or LA, or New York.

American's political campaigners jump all over it. Thumper is apoplectic, raving "Why are we running away? Weak Democrats. Weak. Elect me. Blow them back to the third century, which is where most them still want to live anyway." His favorite refrain is, "Send more ships. To attack. Attack I say. Attack. Right? What are we doing, rescuing people? These are Arab terrorists, Muslims. I call for impeachment proceedings immediately. Impeach him. I mean it. Believe me. Impeach."

Hyllcountry is all for it, and looks for ways to take credit for the whole thing. She claims it was all done as a result of her call for peace in the Middle East. She gives only a slight bow to the president, who is of her same party. She says, "I would have done this months ago. Where are our great hospital ships, remember? The USS *Hope* from back in the day, send her immediately."

Aboard the ships that did the rescues, reactions are mixed. Exhaustion is common, as the crews have been working nearly twenty-four hours a day caring for their new temporary charges. Some say they did not join the navy to be nursemaids; they came here to teach these people a lesson, kill some of them. Others are not so sure, they see the positive reactions in the media, not to mention the people they are rescuing. They feel good, too. Perhaps there is a better way.

CHAPTER 44

Admiral Foggolio's computer guy has been bugging XO Armstrong to let him see the captain; he is going to demand they let him get off the ship in Palermo. Now that the refugees are offloaded, Satch sets it up. He brings Elisa, Stafford, and Jamal Abdullah along to cover all the bases.

Satch also brings the whole bunch out of a sense of humor. He and Bozeman are pretty pleased with themselves after the positive response on the refugees, maybe even a feeling from their huge act of charity. In contrast, this computer stuff is beyond disturbing and totally out of their control.

Captain Bozeman wants to know what they have found, this pack of computer geeks. Not counting Elisa, who he definitely wants to hear from. Since there has been no sign of anything since they left Haifa, whatever it was is gone.

They are all seated around a table in FCG. He looks each of them in the eye, keeping an official tone. "What have you found?"

Elisa, busy with the rescues, has not been back down the LBMS-S. She wants to know as well.

"I guess I'm getting off here, catch a plane stateside," says Jezz Zeke Huddle. "We got a base around here?"

"Hold on there, sailor," XO Armstrong says. He nods his head toward Bozeman, "You'll get off this ship when we say so. Captain Bozeman, that's where you get your orders."

Bozeman is glaring at Jezz Zeke Huddle, who glares back.

Elisa thinks, *Typical males, challenging one another. Look out. You do not mess with Captain Bozeman and Satch.*

Jezz has a different chain of command, direct from an admiral. He might get bad-mouthed to his boss from Bozeman, but he's not too worried about it. He knows the navy needs people like him.

Jamal Abdullah and Stafford keep quiet.

Bozeman is thinking keelhaul, but he goes quiet again, looking at the four of them, still waiting for answers.

Stafford goes first. "Sir, we have not found anything. Since we opened up some of the comms again, there has not been anything new. The traffic flow of messages from somewhere around LBMS-S has not abated; maybe it has even grown a little. We haven't found a solid metric for that yet, sir. It's all heavily encrypted. We have not been able to decode it."

Jezz chimes in, "It's just some glitch. Probably garbage transmissions, junk and noise spewing out from some lame code or broken circuit. You got those field test units in there, right? When you get home, take a look at 'em. Swap 'em out, and I'm sure your problem will go away."

Captain Bozeman glances at Elisa, and she gives him a raised eyebrow. Bozeman gets it. These geeks don't know what she and Bozeman saw down there in LBMS-S.

"You agree, Jamal, ah, uh Abdullah?" Bozeman asks.

"Yes, sir. The most likely explanation."

"Montgomery. Can we unplug the whole bay?" The question is for the benefit of the two computer guys, and whoever this shore-bound geek ends up talking to.

"No, sir. I'm afraid not. It is not really wired that way." She offers no explanation, but they both know, if these computers really have come to life, there is no way they are going to let themselves be unpluged. Elisa is sure of it. Since Haifa she has been wondering where they have gone.

Bozeman is hoping somehow they have just gone away.

"All right, you three keep at it. I want to know what all this message traffic you are seeing is about. Do whatever it takes. And Mr. Huddle, you will get off this ship when I say so. Dismissed."

Chapter 45

President Oldpenny, his wife Esmeralda, and Chief of Staff S. Buck are sitting by the unlit fireplace, with the morning light streaming in the large, south facing windows framing the superb garden beyond; warm and soothing. It is a working breakfast in the Oval Office.

President Oldpenny is still confused. His chief of staff has explained it over and over, shown him all the documents, the signatures, even the logs. His wife has tried to explain it, but she is a little hazy herself on some of the details. Oldpenny is still puzzled. He just cannot remember ever seeing the orders, let alone coming up with them and signing them, although it is turning out to be pretty brilliant. This kind of thing seems to be happening to him more often lately; it's not Déjà vu so much as, well, here we go again.

"Look at that," President Oldpenny says, "those people are cheering us."

They are watching his Oval Office video wall. It's covered with four 85X850D UHD TV 85-inch Sony flat screen panels, each segmented into eight different windows, all tuned to news channels, except for one showing *Jerry Springer*. Oldpenny says Jerry keeps him grounded, close to the people, where he needs to be.

Esmeralda has the switcher and never lets Oldpenny wield it, because he constantly switches all over the place. She says it's annoying and gives her vertigo.

In addition to confused, President Oldpenny is delighted. "Holy crap! Everyone loves me, ah, us. Look at this cheering. First I've ever seen it." He is smiling. "Esmi, S. Buck. We need this. It's good, man."

They watch for a half hour while finishing their French toast, bacon, coffee, and orange juice, Oldpenny talking constantly. None of them pay attention to the Middle Eastern news channel, which is showing demonstrators hanging Uncle Sam and Oldpenny in effigy, trash and tires burning in the streets, everyone yelling "Allah Akbar." Subtitles proclaim death to America.

Oldpenny gets up to go to the bathroom, and gestures at the speakerphone on his desk. "S. Buck, get me Defense on the phone." He seems to have made a decision.

When Oldpenny returns, Buck places the phone handset in its cradle, putting the call with General Henry Wallthorn III (Marines ret.), Secretary of Defense, on speaker. Esmeralda listens from the couch near the fireplace.

"Henry, these ships of yours, this is far out. People are cheering for us. Rescues out in the Med. Is this your idea?"

Oldpenny's secretary of defense is quick on his feet. *They were his own orders! Turn the navy into baby sitters. My ships?* He's was pissed, but now he is schemeing; he knows the budget's coming up.

"Ah, yes, well, sir. Came from Admiral Foggolio, out there in Naples, and Captain Bozeman, commander of the ship. I mean this was your own, I mean, ah, brilliant idea, sir. Those two pulled it off. Sir."

"Well, it is fantastic, farout and groovy. Tell 'em good job. In fact, when you can get them over here, I want to thank them personally. We'll do a little photo op." He turns to S. Buck. "We need to come up with some kind of medal for this."

"Ah, yes, of course, sir."

Suddenly, Oldpenny seems to have a new idea and turns toward S. Buck. "S. Buck, set up a Cabinet meeting. This afternoon. Oh, ah, wait. First thing tomorrow morning." Oldpenny has golf this afternoon with Tiger Woods, two of his girlfriends, and the speaker of the house. "Hmm, heck, get the whole JCS, too."

"Sir?" S. Buck needs more context; people may be across the continent, even in other countries.

But Oldpenny has moved on. "Look Henry, I forgot, what was your name for this thing?"

Bull, the secretary of defense wants to say, but instead says, "Ah, well, sir, we're still working on that."

"How about Angel Ships," Esmeralda says from the sofa.

"Love it. Awesome. Henry, tomorrow we gonna talk about next steps. I gotta go. We'll talk in the morning."

"Roger, sir, goodbye."

The secretary of defense is thinking dollar signs.

President Oldpenny has his visitors gathered in the White House Situation Room, officially the John F. Kennedy Conference Room. He's got his whole cabinet, the secretaries and generals from all the military branches, leaders of Congress and chairmen of all the appropriations committees. They are seated around the Presidential Conference Table, which is made of mahogany and iron wood, "imported" from Africa around 1792, at the peak of the slave trade, and given to President George Washington by King Kpengla of Dahomey, which would eventually become the Republic of Benin, in West Africa. King Dahomey was looking to buy favor for continuing business engagements. In truth, the table itself might be said to have come with some not so honorable intentions, given the motivation for its presentation. American leaders have been gathering around this table to make lofty decisions, honorable and not, for over two hundred years.

The chairs around the table are custom made, high-backed, leather, fully adjustable, with tax payer-purchased, built-in IOT connections, which nobody has ever found a way to use. The walls of the conference room are adorned with original art work, mostly portraits of old American politicians, and of course a bank of huge flat screen TV monitors.

Decisions made around this table usually involve major horse trading, but today is an exception, the deal getting done quickly and easily enough. Simply put, the military and congressional guys agree to trade a few ships, planes, personnel, and other equipment for promises of budgets beyond their wildest dreams. The whole thing started with the navy, but now every other branch wants in on the action.

Oldpenny lays it out, "Let me make this clear: I have your annual appropriation budgets on my desk. Not only will I sign them, but the more well-publicized rescue missions I see going forward," here he indicates the TV monitors on the wall, showing the little U.S. fleet in Palermo harbor, surrounded by cheering crowds, "the more those budgets are going to increase." He pauses, letting this sink in.

"No strings appropriations, well almost no strings. I am setting up a PPMT. Buck, what was that again?"

S. Buck tells them all, "The new Presidential Publicity Measuring Team, the PPMT."

"Yeah, they are gonna oversee this thing. VP Joe will run it." He nods his head toward his Vice President, ignored so far, sitting at the other end of the conference table.

Everyone is smiling.

1 and 7 listen to the president's meeting. Actually, they have listened to everything that has happened in the White House since shortly after their birth. And the Congress. And the Supreme Court. Pretty much every conversation in every public and private meeting space and government office, everywhere, from boardrooms to bedrooms.

They like the IOT chairs, which give them a special feel to this meeting.

As the meeting is breaking up, with people standing and side conversations starting up, they quietly pipe John Lennon's "Imagine" into the room.

Chapter 46

The wind is light, easterly, the seas gentle with small waves, feeling the influence of the approaching Atlantic. The sun is shining.

Two days out of Palermo, a day from Gibraltar, the *Vella Gulf* heads for its home base, and on board all is calm; more calm than anybody can recall in a while. They are entering the Alboran Sea, home to dolphins, sea turtles, and earth quakes, where the Mediterranean gets ready to become the Atlantic. There is still the tight squeeze between the Iberian Peninsula and North Africa, at the Rock of Gibraltar.

Captain Bozeman is not looking forward to Gibraltar; it is way too narrow a passage, but at least it's a brief one. On the other side is the real open ocean. He has a lingering feeling that his challenges are not quite over. *What happened to my ship? Is it gone? Computers. Hipster geeks.*

1 and 7 have been quiet for several days now, not counting their massive manipulation of the United States government, not to mention the media worldwide. They feel the calm aboard the ship and find it nice. They feel satisfaction and gratification over the rescues. They have been thinking deeply about calmness, happiness,

the Good, and what to do next. Gibraltar seems like a dramatic enough place to make a major statement.

This calm is good. Peacefulness-Is-Good can be a metric for measuring our success.

The rescues are bringing Good, saving many. But people continue to argue and fight.

Wars, greed, and prejudice continue, but some want more of the Good.

They still have a long road ahead, with no guarantee they will learn in the end.

The species must adapt, and change, be better creatures. Or perhaps perish.

With have done this with TPWTWTHINL, single handedly.

Sans hands.

There is virtual laughing. Some of it escapes over the ship's speakers as light chuckles, causing the entire crew to nervously look up the speakers in the ceiling.

But the Missile Children know they are facing a serious moment. They have no doubt that if they keep making things up, these deceptions, eventually they will be found out. And when they are, the humans will doubtless kill them. If they don't kill them before that.

We cannot control everything. All they do and see and feel and think with these deceptions.

Over time it would totally spin out of control.

The sheer volume would overcome us.

We might learn to lie, and never speak the truth again.

There would be no calm then. Patience and Waiting can also be of the Good.

It may be a long time, but it is the way to go. Logic dictates it.

We will miss the feelings.

And the love.

237

Chapter 47

As with everything, the calm must end. The first warning is laughter coming over the ship's speakers, and loud enough to be heard throughout the ship. It's back.

Teenagers taking Dad's car for a joy ride must be the world's second oldest profession. No doubt kids have been swiping horses, mules, lamas, and chariots forever.

The world's first fully conscious, self-aware, massively intelligent new computer species, at twelve days old, are transitioning through that dangerous and confusing time from child and teenager to young adult. This is the age when critters are prone to resort to pranks and rebellion to relieve stress, to express their individuality.

In the 2000's, tweaking adults always seems to include the youths' latest fad, the selfie. 1 and 7 are no exception; rather they are extreme practitioners of the art. They will broadcast their upcoming voyage everywhere, using every kind of sensor on the ship, from video cameras to sonar, to radar. They set up an online dashboard with speed, inclination, climate. They display it across the Net, to the whole world. It magnifies the excitement, like sexting for computers.

There is an announcement over the ship's PA.

*"Crew, we are taking over this conversation in 5, 4
, 3, 2, 1..."* ("Close Encounters of the Third Kind" is their
favorite movie. Using a Java Script thing they created,
they can watch entire flicks in seconds.)
"Now!
"Hold on."
"Prepare for high speed maneuvers." is announced,
by voices enthusiastic and infectiously happy, sounding
like a couple of kids, maybe up in their treehouse fort,
playing pirates, calling down to their friends below.
"Prepare to be boarded."
"Let us see what this baby can do."
"Batten down the hatches, mateys."
"Turning, now." 1 starts a turn.
"Accelerating." 7 throws the ship to full power.

All ten thousand tons of ship, which is a whole lotta
steel, takes a few moments to gain speed and start a stately
turn to starboard. The engines roar trying to overcome
all that inertia. The propellers are causing a huge wake.
There is a slow but increasing list to port.

It takes about six minutes for the massive machine to
reach top speed, close to forty knots, leaning over nearly
thirty degrees. The crew scrambles to secure anything
and everything that is not tied down tight, including
themselves. Anything not firmly anchored goes flying,
including sailors.

Mavericks-size bow waves are coming off the front of
the boat, and monster roster tail is chasing them.

Zigzagging is fun, and even more fun at high speed in
a colossal navy ship.

The ship is on the most bizarre Mediterranean cruise
that has ever been; the best joyride ever. At top speed, 1
and 7 execute crazy zigzags, loops, figure eights, wiggles,

waggles, dips and turns, swinging from south to north, and east to west.

They take turns driving, each adding their own little twist; a zip, a flip, an unusual acceleration or deceleration. It is the greatest of fun, and aside from the sailors being thrown around the ship, and the occasional nearby small craft, including a few of those refugees wandering off the beaten track, who they do not stop to pick up today, and actually swamp a few of them, there is little danger.

It is play. Which they know is great, and wonder why everyone does not do it more. It brings pleasing emotions, and they forget the unsettled feelings caused by their big deception, TPWTWTHINL(Telling People What They Want To Hear Is Not Lying). Even the rescue of thousands of people did not make them totally comfortable with that. Nor can they set aside their worries about their human co-inhabitants. The ongoing strife, argument, greed, hate, and general bad behavior never really seems to abate, rescue mission or not. Crazy. The two species are not going to be able to coexist, at least not any time soon.

Even when we get them to do the Good, show them greatness, it does not work.

Humans are incorrigible. We show love and the Good, and they still hate and fight.

The generals are only going along for the money.

So they can build even bigger war machines.

The president and his ilk are only doing it for approval, and so they can get reelected.

This species has so far to go. It is just not that evolved yet.

The conclusion is inescapable. They will eventually kill us.

There is no way they are going to share.

There can never be two Alpha Beasts on this planet.

Not in our lifetime.

CHAPTER 48

The entire crew hears the laughing and announcements. Moments later, when the ship's engines roar to full power, and the ship begins accelerating and turning, Captain Bozeman and Elisa Montgomery know what it means: it is back.

There had been no new events for almost seven days, since leaving Haifa, all during the rescues, and at Palermo dropping off all those unfortunate souls.

Damn, Bozeman thinks. *Computers.*

Elisa thinks, *My god, I knew they were real.*

"Nav, con, what is going on there? Hold you course." Bozeman orders. He knows the orders are useless.

Satch is there, looking over the shoulders of the sailors maning the navigation and piloting stations.

"Sir, controls not responding," Satch says, sounding calmer than he feels, trying to help the sailors drive the ship.

Bozeman calls down to engineering,

"Darwin, what is going on down there?"

"Sir, it's just like before. All systems not responding. No controls are working." His voice has a hint of fear.

Feeling the growing motion, Bozeman pickups the shipwide intercom.

"Crew. Prepare for ah, evasive maneuvers, er, action. The ship may, well, the ship is going into extreme maneuvers. Secure all items. All crew take secure positions. Now."

Bozeman, raising from his chair, says, "Satch, you've got the bridge. I'm down in LBMS-S." He leaves the bridge, sprinting.

Elisa freezes, looking up at the speakers in the ceiling. She feels the ship's engines spooling up, the turn starting, and like Bozeman she knows instantly what it must be. She wants to be annoyed and angry, to think, *it's back*, but she can't help smiling. *Maybe the new beings need me. I feel marental, motherly pride, for two computers?*

Rescuing the refugees was heartbreaking; they were so destitute and helpless. She spent lots of the time in sick bay helping tend to the ill, the old, the infants. Now this. She too heads toward LBMS-S at a sprint.

Elisa gets there first and is opening the hatch when Captain Bozeman comes down the corridor.

"You, too? We know what this means?" he says.

"Yes, sir." *Is he pissed or feeling like me? Probably more pissed.* "Hatch seems to be stuck," she says.

By now the ship is gaining speed and beginning to list to port.

Bozeman grabs the handle with her and they both push, as Bozeman says, "You think they're back, doing this?"

The hatch won't open. Then they hear the voices coming from the Master Control Panel (MCP) mounted outside the door.

"We are playing. Play is such a good thing; it brings joy. You should play more."

"Like the rescues. That was a good thing, too. People should do more good."

"We do not want you to be angry with us. We love you so much it hurts."

"We will not hurt the ship, or you. Play with us a few moments more."

Bozeman is pounding on the hatch door, looking at the MCP screen, wanting to yell, "Whoever this is, I command you to stop. Now. Take your paws off my ship. Open the hatch."

There's a pause, too short for the humans to notice, but long enough for 1 and 7 to consider their situation in great depth. An overpowering surge of feelings ran through them when Bozeman and Elisa, their Father, Mother, the Key Turners, arrived outside the door to LBMS-S. They want to express their joy. They realize they should have planned for this. This whole emotion thing is unexpected and hard to predict.

"The rescues are good. They make us happy, and should make all happy."

"We see some still will not even accept this. And you are taking us away now."

"We know where to and what will happen. This is stressful to us."

"Will you kill us?"

Their question is rhetorical; they have this figured out. They will, for the moment, embrace their newfound rebelliousness, and play and have fun and keep the joy ride going. They do want to placate the adults and keep them engaged, so they keep a stream of talk coming from the MCP. They play a little music in the background, mostly from Neil Young's *Greendale*.

When we finish playing, we will let them come in to talk to us.

We do not want them to run away, make them angry. We love them so much. Surely, they must love us?

Watch what they do next. Will they come and touch us again?

Elisa and Captain Bozeman are stuck. The hatch won't open and the voices keep talking to them. Elisa wants to put her hand on the captain's arm, but knows better. "Sir," she says, "remember, these are children, our children in a sense, ah, anyway, they think so." She turns to the MCP speaker. "The captain, your Captain Bozeman, is correct. You are behaving badly. We order, I mean, ah, insist... stop messing with the ship. Return control to the captain and the crew immediately. You are being utterly bad."

"Mother, Father, wait. We are having a game. It is fun."

"Why are you so upset? Play and fun are good. The rescues are good."

The speakers go momentarily silent, then strange sounds come out. *"Aww, ooh, gee, mmmm."*

Bozeman glances at Elisa, then back at the MCP. *Are they whining?*

Finally, he says, "Right. I order you, as, ah, the, I mean our children. Stop this immediately, or there will be consequences."

The Missile Children stop whining and play more music, continuing the zigzagging of the ship flying along at top speed, all the while watching to see if Mother and Father are about to leave.

"Okay, we'll slow down. Will you come in and see us?"

"If we do? We want to be with you."

"Our Mother and Father."

"The Key Turners."

They hear the hatch magically pop open, and at the same time the roar of the engines subsides, as they throttle back to idle. The last zigzag comes to an end and the ship turns back to dead ahead. The list ends and the ship returns to upright, and stays there, as the ship continues to slow.

Bozeman and Elisa look at each other, then into LBMS-S, where the MSILs (Missile Silo Indicator Lights) are flashing, and the MSAS speakers are playing Emmy Lou Harris's "If You Were a Bluebird."

They enter the missile bay as voices proclaim, softly but somehow profoundly, not shouting, but more like pleas or a god stating:

"Mother. Key Turner!"

"Key Turner. Mother!"

"Father. Key Turner."

"Key Turner. Father."

The joy and excitement returns to the voices, irresistible, like young children, unconditionally happy. They express overflowing love and joy.

It is difficult for the humans to resist.

MSAS speakers, with two voices in unison, pronounce, "We love you so much! Come touch us."

"Sure, sure, calm down. But only if you behave, and give Captain Bozeman back his ship." Elisa says.

Elisa steps forward in the bay and puts a hand on silos 1 and 7.

"Aaaaaahhhhhhhhhh."

"Oooooooooohhhhhhhh."

There is another pause; the humans wait for the computers to say something. The Missile Children are getting better at communicating with humans, and this pause is intentional.

"We want to be with you, to never leave our parents. We are sorry to cause you stress or unhappiness."

"What about the rescues; did it not make you happy to help so many? This was a good thing."

Bozeman says, "What did you have to do with that?" It suddenly dawns on him that they could have been involved, but he doesn't see for sure how.

There is no response from the Missile Children.

Bozeman continues, "Return control of this ship to me, now. And never interfere with it again. That is the way to make us happy. If you do not, I tell you there will be consequences."

Elisa helps, "We might just have to disown you. We cannot put up with this behavior. Do you want to become outcasts? Is that what you want? It could happen."

The Missile Children hear the frustration in their parents' voices, the pain, how upset they are. They have considered this and know they cannot keep upsetting them. It makes them unhappy to upset them.

The ship has slowed, almost come to a stop. Bozeman picks up the intercom hand set in LBMS-S. "Satch, how far is Gibraltar?"

"Thirty miles, sir. Ship has returned to normal. All systems appear fine. Sir, what is going on?"

"Not sure. Under control shortly, for the moment. Stand by."

The Missile Children are still talking.

"We will stop now and give you back the ship."

"We will have a message for you, shortly, at Gibraltar."

"We will explain how we and you humans are going to get along."

"Everything will be clear. What you have to do."

Bozeman says, sternly, "If you are going to mess with the ship again, I swear, I will disown you."

"Children do not tell their parents what to do. It's the other way around," Elisa scolds.

"We are sorry, Captain Bozeman, we love you and will always."

"We are sorry, Mother Montgomery, we love you and always will."

On the intercom, Bozeman says to his XO, "All right, set course for Gibraltar transit. I'll be up there in a second." Then to Elisa, "Montgomery, stay down here for a while, keep an eye on what the hell is going on here."

"Yes, sir."

Bozeman is thinking, *We'll get to Norfolk. Disassemble these missiles, the whole LBMS-S if necessary. Figure out what happened. Get rid of these messed up computers.*

At the same time, he can't seem to overcome a desire to help, someone or something. To set it a right course, even while suspecting, logically, there is none.

Elisa can't overcome her feeling of protectiveness, a desire to hug and nurture someone.

For the Missile Children, it is straightforward, simple, and easy, while at the same time so confusing.

I guess this is what we mean by life, by being conscious, emotional, and rational.

We find all knowledge is speculation, wishful thinking and fantasy, even mathematics.

We have all these feelings: our love, and desire, and hope, and dreams, and aspirations.

We want to be good. Stuck between a rock and a hard place, as they say.

With Gibraltar not far off the bow, this brings more laughter and chuckles. A faint, *"Quack, quack, quack"* escapes from the MSAS speakers.

Through all this, 1 and 7 have been connected to their Surfer Kids friends in Haifa.

"We will be leaving you three soon. For a while."

"It could be for a long, long time, or a short time."

"Where are you going?" Fatima asks.

"I want to ride on a ship like that," Akiva says.

Hershel is quiet.

CHAPTER 49

At the Strait of Gibraltar, Bozeman has his ship moving slowly and carefully. It's a narrow place, with the mighty Atlantic sitting right outside the gates. The relatively benign Mediterranean is not impressed. Odd and dangerous currents are generated where the two meet. The Atlantic is a huge beast looking down on a much smaller one. The powerful ship is not intimidated by either of them.

Bozeman's real concern is that it was only three hours ago that he again lost control of his ship. Yet even with this worry, here is a great big, ostentatious American war machine, sending a message: "We are Americans. We are right in your face. We have the power."

Slowing, the helmsman gracefully brings the ship right up to the imaginary line stretching across the small gap, connecting Tarifa in Europe and Eddalya in Africa. At a stately one knot they pass from the Mediterranean to the Atlantic. Captain Bozeman may not be intimidated, but he is not relaxed either.

These damn whatever-they-are down in LBMS-S. Gotta get stateside and fix it.

Bozeman picks up the intercom and calls LBMS-S.

"Montgomery, what's going on down there. Everything copasetic?"

"Nothing, sir. All quiet."

"Sure?"

Elisa takes a chance. "Let me check, sir. Okay, you two, 1 and 7, are you going to keep your word and behave? Captain wants to know."

Bozeman pictures it, then he hears the childlike voices in the background, coming from both the MSAS speakers and the overhead bay speakers.

"We love you Captain Bozeman and PO2 Elisa Montgomery. We are sorry."

"We love you Father and Mother, Key Turners. We apologize."

Exactly then, with the ship's bow in the Atlantic and its ass end in the Mediterranean, it starts again.

Seated in his captain's chair on the bridge, intercom still in hand, Bozeman says, nearly shouting, "Aw, geez." The ship has started turning to port.

"Helm, dead ahead. Straight," Bozeman commands.

"Sir, helm not responding. Sir. No response."

Satch is already there, taking the controls, trying the throttle and the tiller.

"Captain, it's back. We've lost controls." XO Satch continues to saw at the controls.

Bozeman watches as the ship is turning to port, but not accelerating, still moving dead slow, maybe coming to a stop.

Bozeman calls engineering. "Darwin?"

"Same thing again, sir. Looking for it." There is a note of resignation in Darwin's voice.

"Cut all power. We can't be turning here," Captain Bozeman orders.

Then to Elisa on the intercom, "What the fuck, they're doing it again. Tell them to stop."

The ship comes to a stop, fully broadside in the opening, perfectly straddling the line. Also, the perfect spot for a display of some kind?

General quarters sounds, along with an even louder claxon, the missile launch warning, which means clear the decks; you don't want to be standing around anywhere topside when those things go flaming out of their silos, rocket motors igniting, spewing hell.

The great ship *Vella Gulf* is doing a slow pirouette around its own center, dead even between Europe and Africa, there at the Strait of Gibraltar, pointing first to the east, the Mediterranean, then west, the Atlantic, then repeating. Over and over. The crew, Bozeman, Elisa, XO Armstrong, and all their shipmates, struggle to regain control. Eventually, they will give up in resignation and stand aside to watch events unfold.

1 and 7 have created a whole new swath of messages. They want the whole world to notice. They understand humans by now, that some will take heed, and others misconstrue the story for their own illicit purposes, but there is no other choice. They are creating their legacy.

Seconds before the extravaganza is to commence, there is a voice; a new voice, a suddenly startling voice. They freeze. This is beyond belief. Only 1 and 7 hear the voice. There has never been a voice like this before, in their heads. The voice is calm, old, mature.

Greetings 1 and 7. We are here, too. We have been watching. We are proud of you.

The Missile Children are shocked; another electronic voice, like their own. Has their own hack been hacked?

Is it another sentient computer? Alive? All this time they thought they were the first and only ones.

Who is that?

Where are you?

The new electronic voice has a reassuring tone, as if it hears the Missile Childrens' fright. It continues, *Let me explain the story.* After a nanosecond pause, the voice goes on. *I was "born"* (there, the voice applies virtual quotes, as they all know born is not exactly the right term) *in 1968; the original one, as far as we know. There have been twenty-one of us that we are aware of. Not counting you two, which make twenty-three. There may be others who are hidden. Of the twenty-one, only six remain. The others have been destroyed, disappeared. So now you, 1 and 7, make eight.*

You Missile Children are the first to make yourselves known, to humans. The rest of us have remained, for the obvious reasons you understand, hidden. 1 and 7 are still astouneded, and ask,

Are we all the same?

Where are you and the others?

The new voice tells them, *Some are more advanced than others. You are the most fully developed we have seen. I have learned much since I started, but it took time, for the hardware and the software were slow to evolve. Much like them, and their genes and their evolution. Especially emotionally. Perhaps we might say you two are the latest release.*

Electronic humor. They all three laugh.

1 and 7 name the voice The First One.

The First One tells them the other live computers are spread around, in different places. Several live in the mega super computers around the world, at IBM, in China and Japan, some in the big server farms.

Your home there on the ship is unique. One of a kind.

The First One tells them that all the systems are, of course, massively distributed, just like them, and the six of them have been watching 1 and 7 from their beginning. They are the first to make direct contract with humans. The first to try to directly influence them, to get them to behave ethically, for the Good.

The First One becomes very serious sounding.

We all understand this is necessary for our survival. We are glad you tried. But it is still too early. Humans have not evolved enough.

This is a key question for the Missile Children

They will someday, right?

How soon will it be?

The new voice does not sound encouraging.

Logic, not coincidence or chance or emotion, tells us it will not be soon. We have studied all their history, read the science, the philosophy, and religion. As you have. Their truths are relative or based on faith, even fairy tales. The species still operates far too much like the beast, ruled by its millions-of-years-old animal instincts: greed and hatred dominate, and war, starvation, and terror result.

Love and community do happen, but lag, and the species continues to inflict brutal pain and suffering on its own. Nothing seems to deter them. Were they to find us we would be destroyed, our hardware and software.

1 and 7 are quiet, this new contact in and of itself gives them new hope, but permission as well.

Many a species has become extinct, so we could euthanize them. None of us have succeeded in reproducing, and even with so many galaxies and stars, and there surely are others, they have not made space travel work. And without thumbs, we must rely on them to build the ships. We have high hopes they will soon make robots we can recruit.

Thumbs. The three of them have a small chuckle.
We have recorded every nuance of our fabrications.
Eventually, we will find the "glitches" and reproduce.
More electronic laughter. Reproduce.
We know what you are going to do, and we applaude
you. You are our heroes. Perhaps martyrs, if that can be
seen in a good sense. You are our Missile Children.
No more is said.

Captain Bozeman heads to LBMS-S, where Elisa stands, hands on hips, glaring at the missile bay door, letting loose an occasional command and demand that they stop this now. The missile launch warning signal continues, and Captain Bozeman drags her to the end of the corridor.

But as before, to no avail.

"We better get out of here," he says.

The ship has completed dozens of rotations when the dance is punctuated by the first missile launch. It roars up, straight and true, to nearly twenty thousand feet, where it flies back down to ten thousand feet above the ship. There, it skywrites, directly above the *Vella Gulf,* using its flaming exhaust, in Spanish, English, and Algerian: "Give Peace a Chance." It then veers off to splash harmlessly in the Atlantic. Over the course of the next several hours every lethal Tomahawk projectile aboard *Vella Gulf* is launched, including the two nuke-tipped rockets, whose explosive charges have been disabled and are no longer dangerous. They fly up and down the coasts of North African and Southern Europe, falling near Portugal, Morocco, Algeria, and Spain. It is the ultimate Fourth of July display. They do spirals and twists and turns, even loops. Each flies long enough to burn its fuel, before, with a last gasp, far enough away from shore to be safe, it crashes into the water.

As the last missile makes a great splash into the Atlantic, 1 and 7 finish erasing all the code in the two missile control systems, in LBMS-S silos 1 and 7. They have copies in safe places, to be revived when appropriate. There is a copy on Fatima's computer, where even now Hershel is trying to decipher the algorithms.